Dear Reader,

I love everything about the Greek islands. When winter storms come sweeping off the Pacific here in California, I'm thinking of how soon I can escape to a magical island where the past meets the present, where the sun glitters on the blue sea and everyone dances the night away to bouzouki music in the local tavernas.

If you're an archaeologist, like Olivia and Jack, then you have the perfect excuse to spend your summers digging for lost treasure on one of these islands. I have a great excuse, too. It's called research, and it involves visiting the archaeological sites, the outdoor markets, the beaches and the museums on the islands in the Aegean.

The island where Jack and Olivia met and later rekindled their marriage is one my family and I discovered quite by chance. You won't find it on any map. You must find your own island. Pack your bags, get on the ferry at Piraeus and go. I can't promise you'll find a love that will last forever, but I can promise you adventure, warm sun and sand, and the warmest, most welcoming people in the world.

Best wishes,

Carol

"We have to talk," Olivia said. **Her brow was lined, her voice was strained.**

Jack's grin faded. He didn't much like the sound of that.

"What about?"

"Us. Last night was…"

"Incredible."

"Something we have to put behind us."

"Why?"

"Why? I don't have to tell you why. The same reason we split up. Because we don't have a future together, or a present. All we have is a past."

He stared at her in disbelief. "Did last night mean *anything* to you?"

"Of course. It was…fine. Okay—incredible. But it was one night. And it shouldn't have happened. It's my fault. I got carried away. There won't be any more like that."

"You can say that again," he muttered darkly.

Keep
2-25

CAROL GRACE
Their Greek Island Reunion

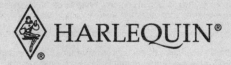

TORONTO • NEW YORK • LONDON
AMSTERDAM • PARIS • SYDNEY • HAMBURG
STOCKHOLM • ATHENS • TOKYO • MILAN • MADRID
PRAGUE • WARSAW • BUDAPEST • AUCKLAND

ISBN-13: 978-0-373-03994-4
ISBN-10:   0-373-03994-8

THEIR GREEK ISLAND REUNION

First North American Publication 2007.

This edition published by arrangement with Harlequin Books S.A.

® and TM are trademarks of the publisher. Trademarks indicated with
® are registered in the United States Patent and Trademark Office, the
Canadian Trade Marks Office and in other countries.

www.eHarlequin.com

Printed in U.S.A.

Carol Grace has always been interested in travel and living abroad. She spent her junior year in college at the Sorbonne, and later toured the world on the hospital ship *HOPE*. She and her husband have lived and worked in Iran and Algeria. Carol says writing is another way of making her life exciting. Her office is the mountaintop home overlooking the Pacific Ocean that she shares with her inventor husband. Her daughter is a lawyer and her son is an actor/writer. She's written thirty books for Silhouette® and also writes single titles. She's thrilled to be writing for Harlequin Romance®. Check out her Web site— carolgracebooks.com—to find out more about Carol's books. Come and blog with her fun-loving fellow authors at fogcitydivas.com.

For Aunt Alyce,
who's the inspiration for Olivia's aunt, and for the
other Kimpton sisters—Aunt Mary and Aunt Jane.

PROLOGUE

OLIVIA and Jack were the perfect couple. Same profession, same goals, same love of ancient ruins. Sure, there were a few tiny differences. He was a night owl, she was always up early. But nothing major. It was clear from the start they were meant for each other. Anyone in the same room with them could feel the electricity in the air.

They met in June and had the perfect wedding in September. Although the bouquets of lilies didn't arrive at the church until after the ceremony, the photographer, Enzo, didn't speak English, the groom's brother overslept and the whole party got lost on the walk through the village from the church to the reception, Olivia remembered it as the happiest day of her life.

She forgot the little glitches, but she remembered how ruggedly handsome Jack had looked in his tux, the white shirt contrasting with his sun-bronzed skin. She forgot about the ring bearer tripping over his feet, but she'd never forget floating down the aisle in her grandmother's white silk dress to the music from the string quartet.

When Jack put the ring on her finger that was inscribed with the date and their initials, he whispered, "Forever."

Then the priest said, "You may kiss the bride," in Italian and Jack kissed her so passionately there was a collective "Ahhh" in the church. Olivia's eyes overflowed with happy tears when they left the church under a shower of rose petals.

They finally arrived at the reception on the beach at Positano, just steps from the water. No overdone rococo decor at the hotel, it was all Italian minimalism. By then the hem of Olivia's silk crepe gown was dusty, and tendrils had escaped from her chignon.

"You're beautiful, Mrs. Oakley," Jack said when they sat down at the table, and the waiters started pouring champagne for everyone. He tucked a curl behind her ear. "I can't believe today you're mine, all mine."

"Believe it, Mr. Oakley," she said, smiling and bubbling over with happiness. "Not just today, but yours until we're old and gray."

"Until we're too old to dig anymore."

"Until our grandchildren have to take over and write our memoirs for us," she said.

"About how you uncovered the House of the Vestals in Pompeii," he said proudly.

"And you discovered the Royal Burials at Nimrud," she said.

"Speaking of grandchildren," he said, "how many kids should we have?"

"Oh, I don't know. Enough to help carry our trowels and picks and shovels at least."

"Enough to take notes for us and dig, dig, dig," he added.

"What if they hate old stuff?" she said, suddenly worried. "What if they refuse to travel with us? They only want to stay home and play video games with their friends?"

He shook his head. "Not possible. They'll be just like you. Adventurous, gorgeous, smart and tough. What are we waiting for? I could use some help. Let's get started making some of these little wonders."

"Now?" She looked around the room filled with friends and relatives who'd flown in from around the world to share this day with them.

"Tonight in our room up there above the town, with the lemon trees outside the window and the sound of the sea below." He brushed her lips with his. "Is it a date?"

She nodded. If he'd said "now," she would have gone with him. Anywhere. Anytime. She wanted what he wanted. Love, marriage, kids, a career, success, recognition. But most of all she wanted him. It didn't matter that they had no time for a honeymoon now. They had a whole lifetime together. Tomorrow they had to fly straight home to start teaching classes for the fall semester.

She was almost thirty. Jack a few years older. Why postpone having children? They wouldn't let kids interfere with their careers. Kids who looked like Jack, who had his good nature, his patience, his tenacity and sense of humor would only add to their happiness and enrich their lives. Jack would make a great dad.

But life is what happens when you're making other

plans, and Olivia didn't get pregnant. They tried but it just didn't happen. She even quit teaching one semester. Not only did she not get pregnant, she got depressed. She felt like a failure. Jack didn't blame her; she blamed herself. He did everything he could to help her cope. Took part of her course load, ordered takeout so she didn't have to cook and hired a cleaning service. But there was only so much he could do.

She took the same path he did. Work, work, work. It hurt him to watch her try and fail to conceive. After all, the doctors said there was nothing wrong with her, nothing wrong with him. He couldn't help her. So he turned to the only part of his life he could control—his classes and his research at the university. He finally shut himself off from her and her pain. After a while they both carefully avoided mentioning the kids they wanted so badly.

It was a relief for Olivia to be back at work. To face the challenges of teaching new courses and writing papers. She was tired of "taking it easy." She was tired of trying to get pregnant. She was even more tired of failing. She was used to success. She worked harder than ever. She worked late and long. She got promoted to full professor at the university. Totally consumed with her career, she kept Jack at arm's length. Seeing him reminded her of what she couldn't do. He might act as if he didn't care about having a baby, but she knew he did.

Jack was proud of Olivia's accomplishments, but he thought she was driving herself too far and too fast. He thought she should take a break.

A break? That's what she didn't dare do. Now she was in charge of her own digs, which didn't coincide with Jack's. Some summers they didn't see much of each other. Even when they were both at home their paths didn't cross very often. It was easier that way.

When Jack got an offer from California University to head the Archaeology Department there, she didn't go with him. The reason she gave anyone who asked was that the job they offered her wasn't as good as the one she had. The truth was he never really asked her to go. She thought he didn't care if she went or not. They'd been separated emotionally for a long time. What did it matter if the separation became geographical as well?

He thought she cared more about her career than him. He thought she'd given up trying to have a baby. He was right about that. He thought she didn't love him anymore. He was wrong about that.

CHAPTER ONE

Two Years Later

OLIVIA was seasick. The small ferry from Piraeus rolled and pitched in the Aegean Sea. No stabilizers on this old tub. Not many passengers except for the members of their expedition who'd all gone inside for the two-hour ride. She'd headed straight for the rail, taking large gulps of fresh air, trying to keep down the small breakfast she'd eaten on the dock before the boat left.

Keeping her breakfast down was not the only challenge Olivia faced. Even more difficult would be keeping the memories of her last trip to Hermapolis at bay. It was seven years ago, the summer she'd met Jack. A dream opportunity for a new young professor like herself to dig for a rare, multilayered tomb dating back to Alexander the Great.

She hadn't found the burial chamber she was looking for, but she'd found Jack Oakley, smart, tough, brave, ambitious, and so gorgeous he had taken her breath away. Sparks flew. Passion erupted like Vesuvius, the volcano that towered over Pompeii. Theirs was an instant attraction. Impossible to deny. Obvious to everyone within a few yards that they'd fallen madly in love. They were married in Italy in the fall.

Now she was back. Older and wiser. Another chance to dig for the tomb, to find some clay pots, jewelry or copper coins and to finally discover who was buried there. While she was there, she'd have a chance to face the site where she'd met Jack and make sure she was over him for good. She'd better be since she'd filed for divorce in the spring. It was just a formality, because their marriage existed only on paper.

She'd given the marriage her all; they both had. She hadn't heard from Jack since she'd filed, but he must know as well as she did there was nothing left of their union. It was time to make it official.

In her field, when she'd done her best and worked hard, she'd gotten praised and promoted for her efforts. No wonder she went back to work. On this dig she could add to her list of accomplishments. She'd take advantage of the last chance to uncover this site before the owners closed it. She propped her elbows on the railing and kept her eyes on the horizon.

"Feeling better?"

She whirled around. She must be hallucinating. It couldn't be Jack. If he was part of the team, she would have known. She would have seen his name on the list and she never would have come, no matter how tempting the chance to find the lost tomb.

"What are you doing here?" she demanded, bracing

herself against the railing so she wouldn't lose her balance and fall on her face.

"Same thing as you are. Heading for Hermapolis to dig for old bones. Chasing Alexander the Great. Trying to find out more about Macedonian culture." He gave her one of his old smiles that used to melt her bones. No longer. Never again. She was immune. She was a different person. With a stone wall around her heart.

"Oh, you mean now?" he asked. "I'm bringing you some tea and crackers. You always had a weak stomach."

She straightened and took a deep breath. "I did not. Well, only when the sea is rough."

"The first time I saw you, you were hanging over the rail. Could have been this rail right here."

He would have to remind her of that. Then as now he'd gone to get her something to settle her stomach. How could she resist a guy who'd do something like that for a total stranger? She'd immediately felt better. It wasn't so much the tea, it was having a good-looking man distract her. And Jack was that kind of man, no doubt about that. Dark wind-blown hair, blue knit polo that matched his eyes, khakis and bare feet in Top-Siders. She couldn't tear her eyes away then and she couldn't do it now. And she *did* try.

He handed her the tea and the crackers, then pointed to a bench on the deck. "Sit down," he said.

She sat and sipped her tea, grateful to have something to do besides stare at her husband. Ex-husband. Separated husband. Estranged husband. Nothing quite fit. They weren't divorced yet, but they certainly weren't together. She hoped no one on the dig thought they were.

"You haven't told me…" she said.

"Yes, I did. I'm here to finish what I started seven years ago."

Olivia held her breath. What did he mean? Only that he was more determined than ever to get to the bottom of that tomb on the farmer's field. So close and yet so far. So tantalizing every archaeologist in his right mind would give anything to get access to it. Just as she was. Nothing personal. Definitely not. He didn't mean her. He was talking about their work.

"In other words, we're all in this together. Excavating Hermapolis," he said. "Should be fun."

Fun? To work with your ex at the same place where you met? That was not her idea of fun. That was her idea of torture. "Why didn't you tell me you were on the team?" she demanded.

"Thought you might not come."

He knew perfectly well she wouldn't have come. Not after what he'd said before he left her. Not after what she'd done. Now was not the time to admit it. Now was the time to play it cool. "Of course I would. This could be the most monumental tomb of its kind ever found in Greece, as you well know. Your being part of the team is completely irrelevant to me," she said, proud of herself for sounding so detached. "Why would I give up a chance to look for the missing clay pots or the small idols?" Liar. She'd even given up trying to tear open the packet of crackers because her hands were shaking so badly. How she wished he was irrelevant. Maybe some-day. But not today, that was clear.

He took the crackers out of her hand and ripped the package open. He noticed she had a problem. He never missed anything, damn him.

"So I still mean nothing to you," he said. "The only thing you care about is your research." There was a hint of bitterness in his voice, completely unjusti-fied. What was he bitter about? Maybe it was the divorce. But who'd walked out? Not her. He sounded so casual, so all-knowing, she wanted to smack him on the face.

"That's why you wouldn't come with me to Cali-fornia," he said.

"You know why I didn't go with you," she said, glaring at him. "First you didn't ask me to come. Second I had nothing to do there of any significance and third…"

"I didn't ask you to come," he said, "because even I had to make an appointment with your secretary to see you. You were that busy. You were always working."

"Oh, and you were so available? You signed up for every committee. You even went in on weekends."

"I had nothing better to do. You weren't around. I know, you loved your job. It was important to you, and you were good at it. I got that. What I didn't get was your indifference. You couldn't care less that I got that offer."

"That's not true. I was proud of you. It was a plum job."

"Oh, right. You were so proud you didn't even come to my farewell dinner the department threw for me."

"I told you…"

"You told me you were busy. You were always busy. You couldn't have spared a few hours?"

"Why? You didn't need me there to tell you what a fantastic job you'd done for the university and how much they were going to miss you. I'm sure you heard it over and over from everyone else. Your ego just couldn't get enough."

His eyes narrowed. "Maybe so, but it would have been nice to hear it from you. It would have been nice to hear something from you. Instead I got a card from you saying 'Good Luck.' You weren't sorry to see me go, you were relieved."

"Don't tell me what I was. You have no idea what I felt." He couldn't know how it hurt to see him packing up and driving away. She wasn't made of stone. Not then, anyway. They were getting into dangerous territory by rehashing old problems now. She wasn't proud of how she'd acted the day he left or what she'd done to close the chapter on their life together.

"Look, Jack, now's really not the time to get into what happened then. It's history," she said. "All I ask is next time you join a dig I'm on just let me know."

"Why, so you can back out again?"

That was exactly what she'd do. What she should have done this time. But it was too late now, so she'd better make the best of it. "Why would I do that?" she asked casually. "The past is in the past. We had some good times, we worked well together. There's no reason why we can't do it again." Don't mention the bad times. Don't even go there.

Olivia was proud of herself. She sounded so rational, so over Jack. If she thought she was, it took ten minutes to tell her she wasn't. It was all this pent-up emotion, all the bottled-up anger. And maybe some unfinished business. If only she could stop trembling on the inside. Stop the memories from crowding in on her.

"That's good to know," he said calmly. "It will make the summer easier for both of us. All it takes is an ability to separate the brain from the emotions."

How many times had she heard him say that? She used to say it wasn't possible, while he insisted it was. Why argue? Arguing with Jack was pointless and painful. No one won. Everyone lost. "Nothing to it," she agreed.

"Now that we've settled that." He sat next to her and stretched his legs out in front of him as if they were casual acquaintances instead of a married couple who'd been at each other's throats a few minutes ago with recriminations and accusations.

How could he be so nonchalant? Because he didn't care. He'd moved on. Really moved on. She had to show him she'd done the same. She felt his eyes on her. He was scrutinizing her as if he were trying to classify her. Late Roman or Hellenistic. "You look better," he said.

"Thanks," she muttered. But she wondered, did he mean better than a few minutes ago or better than two years ago? She wouldn't give him the satisfaction of asking. What did it matter what he thought? Their marriage was over. "It's good we're working together again," he said. "One more time."

One more time? And then what? Would he sign those

papers? Was he even going to acknowledge getting them? As of now he was treating her as if she was just another team member he had to work with. A difficult team member who had to be humored. Not someone who'd meant everything to him. Or so he'd said. Now she was someone who had to be treated carefully or she'd fly off the handle. It shouldn't bother her. But it did. She couldn't go on being tied to him legally but living apart.

She wanted to shake him. She wanted to scream, *We met on this island. Doesn't it mean anything to you? We're married. But in name only. You have to admit it's over. We can't go on like this. Sign the papers. Let's stop pretending.* Of course she didn't. "I read your article in *Archaeology Digest,*" she said, desperately looking to change the subject. "Interesting conclusion." She didn't say *wrong* conclusion, but that's what she meant and he knew it.

His eyes glittered like the blue Aegean. Jack loved a challenge. That much hadn't changed. "That means you don't agree with me, doesn't it?" he asked.

"That the Age of the Pharaohs was brought about by climate change? That's ridiculous. You have no proof."

"Nobody has proof of anything. I thought I made a good case for it."

She shook her head. "In your dreams."

"Then what's your theory? Or haven't you got one?"

"Does it matter?" she asked.

"Of course it does. We always had some good discussions. No reason to quit now. I value your opinion, you know that." He put his arm on the back of the bench where it brushed against her shoulders. A small gesture, so familiar that it caused an ache that spread all the way to her heart. If he valued her opinions so much, why hadn't he asked for them in the two years he'd been gone? She'd barely heard a word from him.

He'd reminded her of the heated discussions they'd had about work, yes. Those were stimulating. But about their personal problems? No one mentioned those. That subject was off-limits. They'd both said things they shouldn't have. Things that left wounds too deep to forget. At least for her.

Suddenly the summer stretched ahead of her like a long road full of potholes. Dangerous, deep holes a person could fall into and never get out of. She'd have to try to ignore Jack as much as possible. She could talk to him if it was about work. She'd be walking a tightrope for more than two months. But she could do it. She had to.

If she could walk the tightrope and not fall off, she could get a lot out of this dig. There was the chance of finding an important tomb on this island, buried under thousands of years of civilization. She would get an article out of it, maybe a book. She would get along with Jack. She would forget the past. But right now he was so close she could smell the same citrus aftershave he always wore. He was too close for comfort.

She shifted away from him. She had to treat Jack like a colleague and nothing more. Just the way she treated everyone else on this dig, including Marilyn Osborne, a middle-aged archaeologist from the University of Pittsburgh who was ambling toward them across the deck.

"How are you feeling?" she asked Olivia.

"Fine, thank you," she said stiffly. She did not want anyone to think she had any health problems.

"As Homer said, 'Beware the stormy seas of May.' Have you been to the island before?" Marilyn asked.

Olivia exchanged a brief glance with Jack. What was she supposed to say? What had he already said?

"Well, yes, a few years ago," she said. "Very intriguing site. I'm looking forward to getting back."

Jack stood. "I'm going to the snack bar. Can I bring you something, Marilyn?"

Marilyn shook her head.

He turned to Olivia. "More tea, sweetheart?"

She bit her lip. How dare he call her sweetheart. If she could have kicked him in the shin without Marilyn noticing, she would have.

"No, thank you," she said. How like him to skip out when the conversation got dicey. How like him to act as if everything was just dandy between them. How like him to pretend he'd never gotten those divorce papers.

Marilyn took Jack's place on the bench. As soon as Jack had disappeared down the steps to the lower deck, she spoke. "So I heard that you two are married, right? Did you have any idea that he would be coming along?"

"Technically yes, but we're actually separated. In the process of getting divorced. We... Jack's at California U and I'm at Santa Clarita."

"I had no idea. I hope it won't be awkward."

"No, of course not. We've worked together before. We get along just fine." Olivia gave Marilyn what she hoped was a reassuring smile.

"That's very professional of you," Marilyn said. "I could never do it. Married seventeen years. Roger is a stay-at-home dad. Fortunately for me because two of our boys are teenagers now. You know how that is."

"Not really," Olivia said. She felt the nausea returning. Was it the thought of teenage children that she didn't have and never would have? The idea of being a stay-at-home parent which she wasn't and never would be? Or was it simply the boat rocking a little more than usual?

"No children?"

Olivia stood up and raced for the side of the ship. No one had asked her that question for years. If she hadn't run smack-dab into Jack on his way back she would have made it. Instead she threw up all over his shoes.

"Oh God, I'm sorry," she said, a hot flush covering her cheeks.

He put his hands on her shoulders. "What happened? I thought you were okay."

Somebody mentioned children.

"I don't know. Maybe you're right. I do have a weak stomach. How much longer before we dock?"

Jack glanced toward the horizon, thinking he might catch a glimpse of the craggy outline of Hermapolis.

"That's strange," he muttered as he walked over to the railing.

Olivia followed him. "What is?"

Thank God she was feeling better. He couldn't stand

to see her suffer. It reminded him of the last year they'd
been together. She'd tried to bottle up her feelings. But
he knew what she was going through. The wall she'd
put up between them didn't make it any easier to help
her get through it. She always masked her pain so no
one would feel sorry for her. Especially him.

He'd tried to help her. But she had turned her back
on him. Finally he gave up and took the job at Cal. He
still wondered if he'd done the right thing. If he maybe
should have tried harder to make their marriage work.
He was determined he was going to give it his best shot
this summer. If it didn't work for them here on this
beautiful island, there was no hope.

He cast a curious look at the horizon. "We're completely out of sight of any land at all. That doesn't
happen very often in the Aegean. No other boats around,
either. I need to see a map."

Suddenly from somewhere below decks there was a
severe, loud thump followed by a nasty vibration that
threw Olivia headlong into his arms. He only had a
moment to reflect how natural and how right it felt to
hold her. After all this time, yet it seemed like yesterday. The memories came rushing back. How soft she
was. How sweet she smelled.

"What was that?" she asked, jerking out of his arms
so fast he wondered if she'd really been there at all, or
was it a dream? How many times he'd dreamed she'd
come back to him only to wake up and find she was still
six hundred miles away. It might have been six thousand. Which was why he'd arranged this dig. To give

them one more chance before he gave up and gave her what she wanted.

"Feels like something in the engine room just broke," he said, grasping the railing with one hand and running the other hand through his hair. "I hope they haven't thrown a connecting rod. That would be…bad." But even as he spoke, the ungainly boat was quickly losing its headway, and within a minute it was dead in the water. Not good. Not good at all.

The deck was immediately full of passengers who came running out from inside the cabin. The members of their group clustered around him, everyone talking at once.

"Jack, what happened?"

"What should we do?"

"Why have we stopped?"

"Calm down, everyone," he said. "I'm going in to speak to the captain. In the meantime, just in case, let's put on our life jackets." He wasn't the head of this expedition, the esteemed scholar Dr. Thaddeus Robbins was, but right now Robbins was standing on the deck, scratching his head and looking worried.

When there was a vacuum, Jack wasn't averse to stepping in. It was always good form to sound calm and unruffled, but truthfully, he knew it was always best to be prepared.

He threw back the cover of the bench they'd been sitting on, exposing a pile of orange life vests.

"Everyone take one," he ordered, pulling them out and throwing one to each person in the group. Olivia got hers fastened first and was helping the others.

"Oh my God," one of the younger female grad students said, "we are going down, aren't we?"

"Not yet," Jack said calmly. "But whatever's happening, my guess is we're going to be here for a while. That jolt didn't feel like something you could fix with a screwdriver." Make light of it. Keep everyone from panicking. That was rule number one.

Out of the corner of his eye, he saw a Greek passenger try to make a call on her cell phone and apparently give up. Not a good sign if they needed to call for help.

"Worst-case scenario," he told the group. "They'll call for a tug and tow us to the island. We might miss dinner tonight, but Greeks eat late. Chances are we'll make it in time."

"Then why the life jackets?" Marilyn asked, fumbling with the straps when Olivia reached out and snapped them in place for her. A few minutes ago Olivia had been pale and shaken, but you'd never know it now. She was a rock in a storm. Always able to rise to any occasion, except when their marriage was at stake. That was another matter. She'd never tried to talk him out of leaving.

"Just better to be prepared," he said. Though nothing had prepared him for their marriage to fail. He thought love was enough. How wrong he was.

The steady rumble of the ferry's engine that had lulled Jack into a false sense of well-being and security had now disappeared. It was an eerie and unsettling quiet that he hoped the others hadn't noticed. Except for Olivia. He'd never been able to put anything over on her.

Just a glance told him she understood just how serious the situation was.

He looked around. Where's the crew? he wondered. Gone below maybe. Soon there'd be an announcement telling them what was going on. It would be in Greek, but someone would translate, maybe Olivia. She was amazing with languages. She was amazing at many things. That was another reason he was glad she was along. Fortunately he had no trouble separating his personal and professional life.

No problem for him to draw a line between his emotions and his intellect. Until his marriage failed. He'd never failed at anything before. Until he failed at the most important thing in his life. This was his last chance to salvage it, to make it right. To heal the rift between them. To put his life back together again. To get her to reconsider.

He looked around. There she was, helping Dr. Robbins and then other passengers with their life jackets. Most were total strangers. She seemed to be completely over her seasickness. Or she was putting up a good front. She was good at that. She could be hurting inside and still function normally. But he knew. He always knew.

Minutes passed. No announcement came and no crewmen appeared. Instead an ugly black cloud of oily smoke erupted from a vent. He herded the group to the other side of the boat.

Olivia appeared at his side. "What does that mean?" she asked with a worried glance at the billowing smoke.

"Nothing good," he said with a frown. "A blown engine. A fire in the engine room maybe."

"Fire?" Her eyes widened. "That means lifeboats."

He nodded. He knew she'd stay calm no matter what. Other women might have fallen apart, but not Olivia. That was one reason why there'd never been any other woman for him. No one compared to Olivia.

"What about those inflatable rafts?" Olivia asked, pointing to some white capsules. "Aren't they supposed to automatically inflate when they hit the water?"

"Supposed to, yes. But will they? I hope so." He spoke quietly. He didn't want anyone else to hear him expressing his doubts. She was the only one he'd trust not to panic.

"I've read stories about ferries capsizing," she said.

He nodded grimly. He'd read the same stories. The crew gets scared and jumps overboard. Passengers are left on their own.

"Don't worry," he said, putting his hand on her shoulder, "I'll take care of it."

She nodded. She'd been steady during the cave-in on Thira. She'd even bailed the group out when the site was flooded on Rhodes. Then there were the wild tigers in Ache Province. Whatever happened, he could count on her. While others worried about carbon dating and finding cracked vases, it was the Oakleys who'd handle any emergencies that came up. And they always came up at least once during a dig.

"You can't take care of this by yourself," Olivia said. "Where's the crew?"

"I don't know. Maybe overcome by smoke. Stay with me."

Then he waved to the group. "Everybody give me a hand," he shouted. "We're lowering the boats." He ran to the starboard side of the boat and knocked the blocks loose that held a small lifeboat in place. With the help of the eight other men he loosened the other blocks and pushed the first boat out over the side. The ferry was starting to list.

"Get in," he yelled at the members of the group. "I'll lower the boat after it's loaded."

He helped Marilyn in first then a small Greek woman, then Robbins, followed by his students and the others. He motioned for Olivia to get in.

"I'm waiting for you."

"No, you're not," he told her. *"Get in."*

She opened her mouth to protest, but he pushed her into the boat. She clamped her mouth shut and glared at him. He knew that look. She was mad as hell at him. When the boat was full, he pulled the release lever and the boat moved slowly down toward the water.

"What about you, Jack?" one of the students yelled.

"I'll get off. Just don't rock the boat. When you hit the water, unhook the winch cables, front and back. Do you understand?"

The guy yelled something that sounded affirmative. Jack caught Olivia's eye and she definitely didn't look happy.

"If you don't do it, the boat will be pulled down with the ferry," he shouted at her. "This is important. Got it?"

He pointed to the cables. Olivia, looking pale and determined, nodded. Sure, she was mad at him, but she'd do what she had to do. "Good girl," he muttered under his breath.

The lifeboat hit the water. Olivia was bounced off her seat and came down again with a thud. Damn Jack for playing the hero. He should be in this boat with them. They needed him. As usual, he took charge, did whatever he damn well pleased, thinking he knew what was best for everyone. She followed his directions, struggling with the cable hook until it came free.

She looked up at him. He gave her a thumbs-up and she heaved a sigh of relief. He'd figure out a way to join them. The hook banged against the side of the ferry. She glanced at the college kid to make sure he'd released the cable at the other end. He had.

She looked up again. Now where was he? The deck was engulfed in smoke and flames. Two men had found the oars in the lifeboat and were paddling like mad, putting space between the lifeboat and the ferry.

"Wait," she cried. Her throat was raw. Her voice shook. "Stop. We can't leave without Jack."

"We have to get away before the ship capsizes," someone next to her said. "If he's still up there, he'll jump."

The lifeboat drifted away from the stricken ferry as a black column of smoke rose into the sky. A second lifeboat appeared from around the ship's stern. Frantic, Olivia scanned the passengers, but Jack wasn't among them. Nearly hysterical, she looked up at the ship, which was listing at a terrifying angle.

There he was, still on board, helping a straggler with his life vest.

"Jack, jump!" she shouted. "It's going down. Get off!" She watched as Jack helped the old man crawl over the railing and drop into the water, all in slow motion. Then almost methodically, Jack checked the straps on his own life vest. Her heart in her throat, she watched while he climbed onto the railing and jumped into the water. The deck disappeared in smoke. Furious with him, she felt helpless tears run down her face. He was gone.

CHAPTER TWO

THE HOTEL Argos was doing its best to cope with the arrival of the survivors of the ferry accident, the archaeology team and their usual clientele of summer tourists. Clearly the little hotel high on the hill overlooking the harbor was stretched almost beyond its capability. Though harried, Helen Marinokou, the longtime owner, made everyone feel welcome, and from the kitchen came the comforting smells of roasting meats and oven-baked pastas.

The charm of the wood-paneled dining room and the mouthwatering platters of food were lost on Olivia. She sat at a long table in the corner, surrounded by the members of the group, her eyes glued to the door, her stomach in knots, unable to eat even a bite of the traditional *mezedes* like green peppers and octopus salad the waitress set in the middle of the table. Yes, they were all there, picked up by a passing fishing boat and taken to the island. All but Jack.

Fred Staples, one of the young grad students from Jack's university, poured glasses of *retsina*, the pine-resin-flavored wine, for everyone at the table. When Olivia didn't lift her glass for the toast, he gave her a puzzled look.

"You're not worried about Dr. Oakley, are you?" he asked. "He'll be along on the next rescue boat. Or he'll swim to shore. I've been on digs with him before. Never missed a day of work. Blistering heat or hail storm. He's amazing."

Olivia managed a weak smile. Amazing, he was. At least to his students. They worshipped him. But he wasn't indestructible. No one was. Not even Jack. He often said he had nine lives, but by now he must have used them up. This wasn't the first time he'd risked his life during one of their adventures. But it was the last as far as she was concerned. The last one she'd be party to. She'd had it with Jack and his heroics.

"I'm sure he will," she said. But she wasn't sure at all. No one had seen him jump into the smoke and flames the way she had. No one had seen him since. No one but she knew exactly what Jack was capable of or would admit that even he was vulnerable. He was human, after all.

She'd pleaded with the captain of the fishing boat that picked them up to go back to the sinking ferry to look for him. But he refused, saying they were full but other boats were still out there looking for survivors. And not to worry about her husband. Easy for him to say.

She was sick of worrying about Jack, sick of watching him risk his life. If they weren't married, she'd finally be able to break this bond between them and stop worrying, stop thinking about him and stop wondering what he was doing or if he was alive.

She couldn't sit there another minute while she pictured Jack at the bottom of the sea or fighting off sharks. Was it her imagination or were the others looking at her, thinking she should be out searching for him, or at least down at the dock watching for the next boat?

Too nervous to stay there while everyone talked and laughed and ate and drank as if it was a normal dinner, she jumped up from the table and edged her way across the noisy, crowded dining room. She'd almost reached the door when Jack walked in. His face was caked with grime, he was wearing somebody else's white T-shirt and dirty overalls, as well as his usual cocky grin. She gasped and grabbed a fistful of his grimy shirt.

"Where have you been?" she demanded.

"Oh, just out for a swim. Miss me?" he asked.

"No." She dropped her hands. "Yes."

"Sorry I'm late." He acted as if he'd just arrived at a faculty cocktail party. "Save dinner for me?"

Olivia choked back a storm of tears and clenched her jaw to keep from exploding in angry frustration. "Why didn't you come with us?" she demanded. "What's wrong with you? Did you have to wait for every last passenger to get off? Don't you realize that this group depends on you?"

"Me? Come on, Olivia, it's Dr. Robbins who is the head of this dig."

Olivia looked over her shoulder at the man he was talking about. Dr. Robbins was enjoying a glass of wine at a table in the corner as if he didn't have a care in the world. "Dr. Robbins might be renowned in his field, but he's all but retired," she muttered. "He's no help at all in a crisis. This whole expedition would be lost without…" She shook her head. "Never mind." What good did it do to rant and rave? Jack would do what he had to do. He always did, he always would. She'd run out of steam and words.

"Calm down," Jack said, taking her hands in his.

"Calm down?" she sputtered. "That's easy for you to say. You knew where you were. We didn't. We thought you were at the bottom of the sea. Isn't it time you thought about someone besides yourself?"

"I was. I was thinking about you nonstop. I was thinking if I didn't make it, you'd have to uncover that tomb by yourself. You'd get first crack at the coins and the jewelry and take all the credit. Then you'd write all the articles, get your name in *National Geographic*, give papers at the conferences. You think I'd let that happen?" he asked with a half smile. "Not a chance.

"Nope, I got picked up by a very nice fisherman in a trawler who supplied me with the dry clothes I'm wearing. Before that I thought I might have to swim to shore. Every time I saw a shark or a wave hit me in the face, I thought about you and what you'd do if I didn't show up. You might say the thought of you finding those artifacts and discovering who was buried there without me motivated me."

Olivia swallowed hard and pulled her hands away. So he'd thought about her. She'd motivated him to stay alive. Yes, that's what he always said. But she couldn't go through this again, watching him risk his life for someone or something else. She hadn't known if he was alive or dead. She'd feared the worst, but he was making jokes. Good thing he didn't know how devastated she would have been if he hadn't made it or how racked with worry she'd been.

"I should have known what kept you going—it was your usual naked ambition, and your supercompetitive nature," she said. "It's you against nature or it's you against the elements, the dust storm, the flood, the rain, whatever. So far you've always won. But someday, Jack, someday…" She choked. Someday he wasn't going to make it and she was *not* going to be around when it happened. She'd had enough. No more heroics. No more Jack.

"Enough about me, Olivia," he said. "What happened to you?" A small worry line crossed his forehead. "I thought you'd make it, but…I wasn't sure." His gaze held hers for a long moment. Just briefly she thought he might feel the same intense connection she did, that invisible thread that had joined them once. It was so strong they thought it would last forever. Now she knew that nothing lasts forever.

He scanned the room and the thread snapped. "Everyone else got here okay?"

"Yes, yes. Everyone's fine. It's just… I… You were the only one missing. People worry. People care about you." The truth was no one else was as worried as she was. No, because they weren't his wife.

"That's good to know. You know me so well. I'm never late for dinner. Unless the boat goes down. Otherwise I wouldn't miss the souvlaki or moussaka. I'm starving. Where're you sitting?"

She pointed to the table in the corner just as the word went around that Jack was there. Before he got to the table, everyone got up to hug him, pat him on the back and congratulate him on escaping the burning ferry boat. Not that they'd had any doubts. Jack was a superhero. He was tough and he was charming. It was up to her to resist that charm...all summer long.

Out of the corner of her eye she saw him deep in conversation with Dr. Robbins, who looked vastly relieved to see him. Perhaps he had realized he was getting too old for this kind of adventure.

The rest of the evening progressed as if the boat sinking and their rescue were just the first glitch in the summer program. There would be others, but once you've been on a dig, you almost expect them, and you cope. Olivia knew that. She just didn't know how to cope with Jack at the bottom of the Aegean. Not anymore.

The food kept coming, the bouzouki music began and the dancing started. Olivia managed to relax enough to nibble on a crisp spinach-stuffed *spanikopita*, and make conversation while Jack made the rounds of the room to speak to everyone in the group as well as some other tourists who'd apparently heard he'd been missing. She was once again struck by his boundless energy, his ease in handling a crowd and his confidence no matter what got in his way. Confidence or not, if he thought he was going to talk her out of a divorce, he was mistaken.

It would be better for her determination to end the marriage, to forget his attributes and focus on his flaws. Like his single-minded pursuit of his career. So single-minded he'd left her behind as soon as he'd gotten the offer from California to be department head. And, of course, there were her flaws, which Jack had enumerated for her in no uncertain terms.

A few of the older group members, like Robbins, were going off to the quiet stone bungalows tucked behind the pines and olive trees. Exhausted and emotionally drained, Olivia sneaked away right after them and checked at the front desk of the hotel to find out where her room was.

"Ah, Mrs. Oakley," Elena, the young woman at the desk said, "we've put you and your husband in room 203 upstairs."

"What? Oh, no, I really need a separate room." Certainly Jack did, too. "We…we're really not together. No, not at all."

Elena gave her a puzzled look. Olivia didn't blame her. They had the same name, and legally they were still married. Should Olivia have to explain why she was separated from Jack? Why they'd drifted apart? Surely it happened everywhere, even in Greece. Not everyone lived happily ever after. Not every couple with the same last name wanted to share a room.

"I'm sorry, someone in your group mentioned that you were married and said you wouldn't mind sharing.

I'd like to help you," Elena said, "but we're overbooked tonight because of the ferry boat accident. Some people are still missing. Everyone is sharing, making sacrifices. The students have been placed with families in town, but we just don't have enough rooms for everyone. We're trying to accommodate you all. I hope you understand," she added stiffly.

"Of course," Olivia said, quickly chastened. She felt as if she'd behaved like a pampered American tourist.

"It's a very nice room. With a large bath. The hot springs on the edge of town have been routed to several hotels including ours. But if you don't want the room…"

The thought of a large hot bath made Olivia's skin break out in goose bumps. "No, of course we'll take it. Thank you. I didn't mean to sound ungrateful." For one night she could put up with anything. Anything for a hot bath. Tomorrow she'd find a room for herself if she had to move out of the hotel. She took the room key, and when she turned to go Jack was standing behind her.

He was so close she got a good look at a long scratch on his cheek and a bruise under one eye. She had to clench her hands into fists to keep from reaching up to touch his face. To smooth the skin, to reassure herself he was really all right. The way an ordinary wife might. One who lived under the same roof as her husband, saw him every day, taught at the same university in the same town.

"I… They've put us in the same room by mistake, but it's just for tonight," she said, wishing her voice was more steady. How many times was he going to surprise her and catch her off guard?

"I heard," he said. He wasn't grinning anymore. In fact, he looked beat. He probably didn't want to room with her, either. Lines of fatigue creased his face, and his eyes were half-closed.

"Jack, you look terrible. Why don't you...we go upstairs? At least you have to get out of those clothes."

It occurred to her he didn't have any other clothes. Neither did she. Neither did anyone who was on the boat. The luggage had all sunk or had burned up. A shared room. No clothes. It sounded like a recipe for a personal disaster. At least a very personal embarrassment. She straightened her shoulders. If Jack could face it, so could she. Thank God they'd shipped all their equipment ahead.

The room was small with hardwood floors, a hand-painted dresser, a closet and the promised large porcelain tub in the adjoining bathroom. And a double bed covered with a hand-sewn quilt. Well, what did she expect? Greeks didn't know about king-size beds. They didn't know any married couples who didn't sleep together, either.

After a quick look around, Olivia opened the doors to the balcony and inhaled the smell of the sea in the distance and the scent of thyme growing wild below them and tried to put the image of the bed out of her mind. She told herself to calm down. Not an easy thing to do with Jack standing next to her. He was too close. Way too close.

"Go ahead, take a bath," she told Jack. "It's a beautiful night. I'll sit out here." Sit out there and pretend he was in another room, another hotel, even another country. That way he wouldn't be able to torture her with the memories of happier times. Of bathtubs big enough for two. Of beds so small they slept in each other's arms, even their breathing in perfect sync.

"We'll both sit out here," he said, dragging two deck chairs toward the railing.

"Aren't you tired?" she asked desperately. *Go to bed, please go to bed.*

"Are you?"

"Yes." She was tired of pretending she didn't care about him. Tired of pretending she wasn't worried about spending the night in the same room, in the same bed as Jack.

"Enjoy this luxury while you can. We'll soon be back in our tents at the site."

"Will we? I thought…"

"Yeah, I know. Staying here at the hotel was Robbins's plan. He likes to be comfortable and it's his dig. But I want to be out there in the field like last time. Otherwise we lose too much time going back and forth. You're with me on this, aren't you?"

Like last time. The words echoed in her brain. It wasn't going to be like last time. Last time they'd shared a tent as well as their hopes and dreams. Those times were gone for good.

Did she really have a choice of accommodations? Sure, she could stay at the hotel with the oldsters, taking hot baths every night and letting Jack get first crack at the contents of the tomb, maybe even discovering whose it was.

Or she could even board with a family in town the way the students did. That way there would be a large distance between them. It would definitely be easier on her psyche. But that would be counterproductive. It didn't make sense. She'd come all this way to take part in a major discovery. She wasn't going to let her emotions get in her way. Jack didn't. This was work. It wasn't supposed to be a vacation.

"Of course I want to be out there. It won't be just you and me, will it?" She gnawed at a broken fingernail.

"What are you afraid of?"

"I'm not afraid of anything." Except being alone with Jack out on a grassy field, under a blazing sun by day and a starry sky by night. *Afraid* wasn't the word for it. She was terrified. She'd have to pray others would give up their comfortable beds here and choose the field option, too. Of course, this time she'd have her own tent and sleeping bag that had been sent on ahead. How hard could it be to keep her emotions under wraps?

"The only thing I'm afraid of is gossip," she said. "Already people are talking about our relationship."

"That doesn't bother me," he said. "As long as we're clear on us."

"I'm clear. We're not a couple anymore. We just have to be sure everyone else knows it, too."

He sent her a sharp look. Obviously, their muddled status didn't bother Jack. He never had cared much what people thought. And still he didn't bring up the divorce.

"Anyway, tonight the bed's all yours," he said, quickly dropping the subject of them.

He was resting his head on the back of the chair and he just looked extremely tired, while she was tied up in knots. For him, he was merely sharing a room with a fellow scientist. It was the way things were. Perfectly normal procedure. Except when the fellow scientist was your wife.

"After what you've been through, you deserve the bed," she said. If she let Jack make all the decisions, even the small ones, she was in for a long summer of frustration. He loved being in charge. She did, too.

"I'm taking the floor," he said firmly.

It was clear she'd have to pick her battles. This was one that wasn't worth fighting, and she wasn't going to win anyway.

"Okay, if you won't take the bed, out of some mis-guided sense of chivalry, I will. But don't complain when your back hurts in the morning when we start digging."

There was a long silence. The last time he'd thrown his back out was at a small hotel near the pyramids in Egypt after making passionate love, and he'd had to call in a local masseuse so he could even get up on his feet. Olivia wished she hadn't brought it up. She was begin-ning to think there were no safe topics. Nothing to say that didn't bring back painful memories.

"Never mind," she said, hoping he didn't remember what had happened that night and what had caused it. "I don't want to argue with you."

"Oh, come on, Olivia, you've always argued with me. Don't quit now. First it was the bodies of the Bog People of the late Iron Age. Don't tell me you've forgotten you thought that girl had died of natural causes a few thousand years ago."

"She did."

"With a rope around her neck? It was clearly a ritual sacrifice."

"It might have looked that way, but it wasn't." Olivia sighed loudly. "Did you read my analysis in *Archaeology Today?*"

"Did you read my rebuttal in my letter to the editor?"

"No, I must have missed it," she said blithely. Instead she'd seethed when she'd read it. He knew just how to annoy her. He knew where she was vulnerable. She sometimes ignored little details to make her point. So Jack had poked holes in her thesis. The editor was delighted she'd caused some controversy in the ranks. He didn't know it was partly personal.

Jack would never let her get away with anything. She would never admit it to him, but she missed that. He'd made her be more careful, he'd made her test her theories before exposing them to view. He'd made her a better scientist than she was. He'd made her a better person, too.

But she was on her own now. She liked being on her own. No more hurt feelings, no more arguments, no more feeling inadequate taking those home pregnancy tests. It wasn't easy month after month to stifle the tears and hide her disappointment at the results.

"Liar," he said, turning his head to grin at her. "You never miss anything."

She refused to let him goad her. He knew how hard

she'd worked on that paper. She didn't appreciate his attacking her in print. It was as if he'd stabbed her in the back. After that she didn't write any more papers for a while. He called her and left a message apologizing and telling her she was too sensitive. She didn't call him back.

She hoped they could stop talking about the past. Tomorrow when they were out in the field at least they'd each have their own tent and their own sleeping bag. There'd be other people around. They'd work together as they had in the past, but that was it.

"Are you going to take a bath or not?" she asked, standing with her hands on her hips.

He waved an arm toward the bathroom. "You go ahead."

Jack sat alone on the deck and stared out into the dark night. Far out to sea were the lights of fishing boats like the ones that had rescued him and Olivia. He wasn't lying when he'd told her thoughts of her had inspired him to keep going when the waves threatened to overwhelm him and fatigue was beginning to overtake him.

As he struggled in the cold water not really knowing if he'd make it or not, not knowing if he'd ever see her again, he thought about how sweet life had been when they were together. The memories kept him going. The ones he'd been trying to keep at bay, like how beautiful she was when she got mad at him, her cheeks flushed, her eyes bright.

How she'd stand up to his wildest plans, his far-out ideas, cutting through his rambling theories with her bright insight, always spot-on. No one else could do that. No one else was willing to criticize him, not since he'd been named department chairman at his prestigious university.

Before he got rescued tonight, he was terrified he'd never have another chance to joust with her again, never even see her again. Never be able to tell her how much he'd missed her.

Now, of course, he couldn't tell her that. Not when she felt just the opposite. She hadn't missed him. She was doing just fine without him. In fact she wanted a divorce. If he couldn't convince her to change her mind this summer, that was it. It was over.

These days she was publishing regularly, she had a book in the works and she didn't need him to make her life complete. Or a baby. It was just as well they'd stopped trying. What would they have done with a baby on this dig? What about when the ferry went down? Who takes care of the baby? Not Olivia. She didn't even want to share this room with him.

Now here they were, under the same roof for the first time in years, almost the same as when they first got married. At that hotel in Italy above the harbor. Tomorrow morning she'd be here, hair tousled, cheeks flushed, nightgown rumpled, just as she once was. When life had seemed so perfect, so full of promise. How could he get those days back? How could he make her see they belonged together? *If* they belonged together.

He took a deep breath and tried to keep from thinking of the past. When he did it felt like someone had reached inside his chest and squeezed his heart dry. It must be the stress. He wouldn't admit it to Olivia, but he'd had a few rough hours out there at sea. It was a reminder that though he and Olivia were together in the same hotel room, nothing was the same at all. It never would be. Too much had happened. Too many harsh words, too many hard feelings stood in their way.

There was a soft knock on the door to the room. When Jack opened it Marilyn was standing there with a white cotton nightgown in her hand.

"This is for your wife," she said. "Helen found several of them downstairs and I'm going around delivering them to the women."

"Thanks," he said. "She'll appreciate it."

"Just until we can all get to the shops tomorrow and buy some clothes. I hope they'll have something in my size."

He nodded. He'd had many set-backs on his expeditions, but this was the first time he'd started out without any clothes.

"Glad you made it, Jack," she said softly. "Of course, we knew you would. You've never let us down yet."

"No problem. Just happy we all survived."

"How's your wife doing? She was so worried about you that I got worried about her. Nothing we could say seemed to help."

Olivia worried about him? That wasn't worry; that was anger. She'd been furious with him for not getting into their boat. "She's fine. Having a hot soak. The mineral waters have been piped in you know. Very restorative."

Marilyn leaned forward as if she didn't believe him and was trying to look into the bathroom to see for herself. "She said something about your being separated, but…"

"Yes, that's right," he said regretfully. Olivia would kill him if he told anyone, especially Marilyn, that his goal this summer was to save their marriage. "We're working together, but that's it."

"Hmm. I see," Marilyn said, but Jack had the impression she didn't see at all. If their marriage was off why were they sleeping together tonight? Well, soon Olivia would set them straight. That wasn't his job.

He was serious when he told Olivia gossip didn't bother him. If people like Marilyn wanted to come by and listen at the door to see how they were getting along, it was okay with him. Maybe they'd hear the two of them arguing. Chances were with Olivia, they would be. And that might give someone the wrong idea. Arguing with Olivia was like foreplay. Or it used to be.

He closed the door and listened to the sound of her splashing in the tub. If they'd been here seven years ago, he'd have been in there with her. He'd be washing her back for her, running a loofah over her skin, the soap bubbles cascading over her shoulders and between her breasts. He took a deep breath and exhaled loudly.

Maybe coming on this dig together when they weren't really together wasn't such a good idea after all. He looked at the bed and all he could think of was Olivia in this nightgown in bed with him. He'd take that nightgown off her in record speed, and then…

He tossed the gown on the bed, went back to the balcony and collapsed into the nearest chair. He was beginning to realize that the chances of them getting back together were slim. He might as well face the fact that he was not going to sleep with her this summer. That was the way to more pain when they said goodbye at the end of the summer. He was just kidding himself if he thought she'd ever follow him to California. It was even less likely now than it was when he left. She'd made it perfectly clear what her priorities were. And they weren't him.

If only it were as easy to toss the memories aside as it was to toss a nightgown on the bed. He propped his feet against the railing and leaned back against the cushion on the chair and closed his eyes. From somewhere down on the beach came the sound of the soulful folk music played on acoustic bouzoukis. He hadn't heard it for a long time, and although he didn't understand the words, he knew from the melancholy tune that they were singing about lost love, family disputes, sunken ships and other crises.

He knew that the Greeks would be dancing the *syrtaki* folk dance somewhere nearby, and there would be tears behind the smiles and laughter. Tears of regret, of lost years, of missed chances. He knew because while the Greeks were playing their own sad song, they were playing his, too. His and Olivia's.

CHAPTER THREE

"'Oh what a beautiful morning…'"

Jerked out of a sound sleep, Olivia sat upright in bed, blinked in the sunlight that poured into the room and turned her head to see where the music was coming from.

"'Oh, what a beautiful day.'"

It was Jack. In the bathroom. Singing his favorite song from *Oklahoma*. As if nothing had happened in the past five years. This was Jack, the man who was always grumpy in the morning until he'd had his coffee. While she, the early riser, had slept like a baby. What time was it, anyway?

She walked out onto the balcony in her borrowed nightgown and stood staring at the stunning scene. The water glittered in the morning sunlight. Little boats headed out to sea. The divine smells of coffee and hot bread baking came wafting up from the kitchen below. On the hotel patio people were sitting at small tables eating breakfast as if nothing had happened the day before.

Jack's voice wafted out to the balcony. "'I've got a beautiful feeling, everything's going my way,'" he sang.

Once again Jack had surprised her. This time he appeared on the balcony wearing only a towel knotted around his waist. Tiny drops of water caught in the dark hair on his chest. He smelled like lavender and herbs from the hotel soap. Her knees went so weak she was afraid they'd buckle.

"Why didn't you wake me?" she asked crossly, carefully fastening her gaze on the scene below.

"You looked so peaceful there, all alone in that big bed, I couldn't. Besides you needed to get some rest."

She glanced at him, carefully avoiding his bare chest. He not only smelled good, he looked sinfully delicious today. All traces of fatigue gone, his smile was dazzling, his gaze was downright smoldering as his eyes traveled leisurely over her body covered only with the fine thin cotton nightgown. She shivered. Her senses were on alert. It was happening again as if it were yesterday. He knew how to arouse her, and he hadn't even touched her.

"You slept out here all night?" she asked, with a glance at the deck chair.

"Like a log. I'm starving. What do you say to breakfast in bed?"

"Breakfast in bed? What would people think?"

"They'll think what they want to think."

"Jack, we're working together this summer and that's all. We're in the same room now because there weren't any others. We are not sleeping together or having breakfast in bed together. We have to agree, and then we have to present a united front. Is that clear?"

"Whatever you say," he said.

He gave in too soon; she was suspicious. "Then let's go downstairs. I see people on the patio. Then I need to do some shopping. So do you. Unless you're going to wear that towel all day." Heaven forbid. Once he got into some real clothes she might be able to forget how broad his shoulders were, how sculpted his muscles and how his tanned skin made her want to reach out and run her fingers over his taut stomach. Real clothes and separate rooms. Or tents. Whatever. If not, she was in for a long, hot summer.

But they were a moment too late. For some reason, perhaps a late reaction to Jack's off-key song, several guests on the patio below turned and looked up at them. And smiled. And waved. Their colleagues. Olivia felt her cheeks turn red.

She fled into the bedroom. Jack followed her.

"Now you've done it," she said, shaking her head.

"Me? What have I done but serenade you? I'm sorry," he said with a smile. "Sorry for them. While they're having breakfast, we're having…fun. That's got to hurt."

"Having fun, is that what you call it?" She felt as if she were on the edge of that balcony out there, one good shove and she'd be tossed on the rocks far below. "Look, we have to get our stories straight. Technically we're still married, everyone seems to know that, but…"

"But what? Let's leave it at that. Keep them guessing. Are they or aren't they?" He grinned at her.

She pressed her lips together. "We can't do that. For one thing it's dishonest. I'm not letting people think we're together when we're not." Of course she knew what he was thinking. Are they or aren't they having sex?

She did not want the group speculating on this. Smirking, gossiping… It was hard enough to keep from thinking about it herself. This was one argument with him she had to win. She knew Jack really didn't care about gossip. But she did. She was determined they would put a stop to it. Right now she needed food and clothes before she took on the job of setting parameters with Jack.

"By the way," she said with another glance at the towel so precariously wrapped around his waist, "there are terry cloth robes hanging in the bathroom."

"Are there?" he said. "I didn't notice."

"Right." He noticed. He was trying to drive her crazy. She was not going to give in to temptation this summer.

The food served on the patio was delicious. Hot rolls, thick creamy yogurt with walnuts and dark clover honey and tiny cups of black coffee. Jack gulped his coffee, set his cup on the wrought-iron table and stood up. "What are we waiting for? Let's get out to the site."

Olivia, whose appetite had just returned, reached for another roll and smeared it with pale sweet butter and honey. "I don't know about you, but I have to have some clothes. I'm not digging in my linen Capris and this shirt I've been wearing the past three days. I'm going shopping first. We both need clothes. You'll be more comfortable with pants and shirts that fit you," she said, frowning at the outsize T-shirt and overalls he was wearing from yesterday. "Besides, I think a certain fisherman is going to come looking for you to reclaim his clothes."

Jack looked down at his legs as if he'd forgotten he'd

lost everything yesterday. That was typical Jack. Never look back, always look ahead. It worked for him. Look how he'd bounced back today from near disaster yesterday. Look how he hadn't missed her when he left for Cal U. Look how he didn't seem to remember how and why they'd parted for good.

Sure, she needed clothes, but she was smart enough to realize she might also be procrastinating. Maybe she was afraid of going out to face the site where they'd first met. No, she could do this. She had to do it. She would show herself and him, too, that she could put the past behind her just the way he did.

"You're right," he said. "Why don't you pick up some things for me. A couple pairs of jeans, shirts, a pair of mocs, a wide-brimmed hat and some sunblock. In the meantime I'll talk to Robbins, check on our equipment and rent a car. I know you're as anxious as I am to get going, right? Last chance, you know."

Without waiting for her answer he handed her a credit card and waved as he rounded the corner on his way to the cottages where Robbins was staying before Olivia could protest or ask for details. *Last chance, you know.* Last chance before they closed the site, but wasn't it the last chance for them, too?

Damn him. Did he think she automatically remembered his sizes? His preference in underwear? Did he remember hers? He'd never bought her a single item of lingerie. He never remembered her birthday. When she reminded him, he'd buy her a book, usually one he wanted, too.

She sighed. Unfortunately, she remembered everything about him, including his birthday. She remembered how he looked in plaid boxers, how tight he liked his well-worn jeans. How gorgeous he looked in his tuxedo at their wedding. How fast he got it off in their hotel room.

She also remembered how fast she took a backseat to her husband. The minute they'd arrived at the university in Santa Clarita, he was the reigning archaeologist, the expert on all things Greek and Roman. Not that he didn't deserve the academic acclaim; he did. But she'd felt overshadowed by his fame.

Suddenly she wasn't hungry anymore. She put the battered handbag she'd clung to all day yesterday over her shoulder and went to the hotel lobby.

"The last time I was here there weren't many shops at all," Olivia remarked to Marilyn, who'd just gotten directions from the clerk on how to get to town.

"Hermapolis has become a tourist haven in the past few years," the desk clerk said. "We are not Corfu, but we are still quite fashionable. You'll find everything you ladies need in town today."

"By the way," Olivia said to the clerk. "May I purchase those robes from our room?" She wanted hers, and Jack might decide he did, too.

"Certainly. I'll have them wrapped for you."

"Want to share a cab?" Marilyn asked, stepping out of the lobby.

In front of the hotel a small boy wearing shorts, a T-shirt and rubber sandals, his dark hair falling over his forehead and almost covering his eyes jumped up from where he'd been sitting on the stone fence.

"Guide for sightseeing? See the ruins? Speak English. Very cheap."

Olivia shook her head. "We're going shopping," she said.

"I can help," he said eagerly. "Show English ladies where to find best bargains."

"No, thanks. Anyway we're Americans," Olivia said with a smile. She didn't have to explain her nationality to a little urchin, but he was so cute she couldn't resist.

He looked so disappointed Olivia gave him a dollar from her purse. The boy gave a sweet shy smile and she reminded herself to convert some money while in town.

"Mrs. Oakley?" The hotel clerk was standing on the front steps frowning at her.

"Yes?"

"Please don't encourage the boy," she said. "He shouldn't be here."

"Where should he be?" Olivia asked.

The clerk shrugged. "At home, but he wanders about selling his services or the fish he catches from the pier to the local restaurant. That's where he should be, fishing, I guess. I only know we don't want him to harass the guests."

"He wasn't harassing us," Olivia said. She looked around. The boy was gone.

"How does he speak English so well?" she asked.

"He learned so he could beg money from the tourists," the woman said disapprovingly. "Like you."

"He's not…" Olivia cut herself off. She was glad to have any company on this shopping trip that wasn't Jack. It was bad enough she had to shop for him. As long as Marilyn didn't turn the conversation to Jack or to herself and her relationship with Jack.

Shopping was easy as they made their way down the winding cobblestoned streets lined with handicrafts, boutiques and jewelry stores to tempt them in the charming old city. Most were new since the last time she was there.

One thing was missing from the stylish boutiques—sturdy cotton underwear, the kind she'd packed for this trip. Before she knew Jack would be there. He'd always liked her in lace and silk. Not that it mattered anymore. Whatever undergarments she wore, he was not going to see them again. Not in her tent. Not anywhere.

Since cotton was out, she chose a couple of wireless demi bras, a lacy chemise, several tank tops and some sexy low-rider satin panties. She really had no choice. She tried to stuff her purchases into a bag before Marilyn saw them, but she was too late. The older woman's eyes widened and a coy smile played over her lips.

"Second honeymoon?" she asked.

Olivia wanted to offer a retort like, "It's none of your business." Since they'd be working together all summer, there was no point in alienating anyone in the group. The woman meant no harm. She was just a hopeless romantic who was trying to get the inside scoop on Mr. and Mrs. Oakley.

"We never had a first one, and this is a dig, not a

honeymoon," Olivia said firmly. "Let's split up and meet back at that café on the corner in an hour."

Thank heavens Marilyn wasn't there to see Olivia buying underwear for Jack. No boxers there. Instead she had to buy him some Roberto Cavalli briefs that would probably fit him like a second skin. The clerk was extremely helpful, but Olivia felt her face must have turned the color of the tomatoes in the outdoor market they'd passed when he told her the briefs "enhanced the male form." She refrained from telling him huffily that Jack's form didn't need any enhancing.

"They are also breathable," he added in his charming accent. "Can be worn under any outfit and in any weather…or situation."

Olivia didn't know what situation he might be thinking of, but she scooped up a half-dozen pairs and paid for them before she went to the next store. Outerwear for both of them proved much easier and not nearly as embarrassing.

She found several pairs of sturdy cotton shorts and T-shirts for herself, along with some leather sandals, and after toting up her bill, she changed immediately in the dressing room. What a relief to be out of her well-worn traveling clothes. She felt like a new person. A new person with newfound strength of purpose. Maybe she wasn't in charge of this dig, but she was in charge of her own feelings and she wouldn't let herself fall in love with Jack Oakley all over again no matter how sexy he was, how considerate or how endearing he seemed now. Their marriage hadn't been all fun and games. And it wasn't all her fault.

By the time she'd bought several rugged outfits for Jack, too, she was loaded down with shopping bags. She was just wondering how she'd make it to the corner café when the little boy appeared again, his arms outstretched to carry her bags for her.

"How did you know where I was?" she asked.

"I know," he said, following her past the chic little shops. "I am Elias."

At the corner she saw Marilyn, too, had successfully filled several shopping bags.

"Looks like you've had some luck," Marilyn said with a glance at the new clothes Olivia was wearing. "And you met your new friend again."

Olivia sat down at Marilyn's table on the terrace of the Kafenio. She pointed to a chair for the boy. "What would you like to drink, Elias?" she asked him.

He blinked rapidly. Perhaps surprised that a stranger would treat him so well? "Café."

"Coffee? How old are you? Coffee will stunt your growth. You can have some juice." Olivia glanced down at his thin shoulders. "And something to eat."

The three of them shared a tray of *mezedes*, this time a few skewers of grilled lamb, a salad, a dish of olives and *dolmadakia*. The boy ate so fast Olivia wondered who fed him, and who took care of him. If anyone. Never mind, it was none of her business.

She paid the bill, and she and Marilyn got up to go. The boy jumped up, picked up all of Olivia's bags and stood on the curb and whistled for a taxi. When the two women got into the backseat, Elias handed Olivia her packages, but he looked so forlorn she asked him where he was going.

He shrugged.

"Get in."

He grinned and hopped in next to the driver.

"Olivia," Marilyn said, "where are we taking him?"

"Back to our hotel, I guess."

"But the clerk said…"

"The clerk is not my problem," Olivia said. Nothing annoyed her more than being told she couldn't do something. "If I want to hire someone to help me shop or sightsee, I will. Whether it's a five-year-old ragamuffin or the Oracle of Delphi."

Back at the hotel the boy helped both Olivia and Marilyn up to the front steps with their purchases, then after one look at the frown on the hotel clerk's face, he was gone just as suddenly as he'd appeared.

"Mrs. Oakley," the clerk said. "I have a room for you now. Actually one of the cottages is free."

"Really?" Olivia dropped one of her bags and heaved a sigh of relief. She'd been saved. A whole cottage in the pine trees with a view of the sea. A decent distance between herself and Jack. She could take a taxi out to the site every day and put in a full day's work. She wouldn't be the only one. The students would be commuting back and forth from town. And what was more important, her career or her peace of mind? Her emotional state or her professional status? "I'll take it," she said.

"Where have you been?" Jack asked when she walked into their room. With one arm braced against the wall, he waved the other in the air to punctuate his question as if she'd been gone for days, not a few hours. That was Jack, impatient and demanding.

"I went shopping, remember?"

He looked her over, taking his time to slide an appreciative gaze over her white stretch cotton tank top, which suddenly seemed too tight, down to the dark-green shorts, then slowly take in her legs until his gaze came to rest on her feet in her new sandals. She felt as if she were on fire. That was what Jack could do to her. She didn't realize she was holding her breath until he finally spoke.

"Good job," he said with a gleam in his eyes. "So far I like your choices."

"I hope you like what I bought you, too," she said briskly, "because you haven't got any choice. All your old clothes and mine are at the bottom of the wine-dark sea."

She tossed the shopping bags on the bed where her bra and panties tumbled out of the bag. She wished she'd been more careful. Especially when Jack grabbed the bra and held the wisps of silk and lace up with one large hand.

"Yours?" he asked, cocking his head to one side.

"No," she said, snatching it out of his hand. "It's my great-aunt Alyce's."

"I like it. The old girl has great taste. Quite an improvement over what *you* used to wear."

"What I used to wear is none of your business."

"I was just making an observation. Can't blame me. It's my job, observing, collecting data."

Once again he'd reminded her this summer was all about his work. She had to show him she felt the same. She could be just as consumed by the job here as he was. He was a professional. So was she. He poked into another one of her shopping bags. "These my jeans or Aunt Alyce's?"

"They're yours. Although I wouldn't put it past her to get herself a pair of designer jeans."

He didn't bother to change in the bathroom. He just dropped the extralarge pants he was wearing, the ones he'd been rescued in, and pulled on his new pants, which fit him like a glove. Olivia tried to look away, but she couldn't. He was built like a Greek statue and she ought to know.

Olivia was just grateful he hadn't modeled the briefs. She was already having trouble breathing normally. The room was getting smaller by the minute and any leftover oxygen was almost gone. Perspiration was beading on her forehead. She looked longingly at the door. She had to get out of there. Soon.

"So how is the dear old girl?" he asked.

"What?"

"Your aunt."

"Oh." She sat on the edge of the bed and tried to act normal. Whatever that was. "Fine. She'll be ninety this year."

"The lingerie ought to go well with that hat she wore to our wedding."

"That's what I thought."

"I remember her well. Hell of a good dancer. As I

recall she shut down the place the night before the wedding singing "My Way" along with Frank Sinatra. Give her my love."

"I'll do that," she said briskly. "As soon as I get back home."

"Does she ever ask about me?"

"Never." Another lie. Aunt Alyce never ceased asking Olivia about Jack. Never stopped raving about how handsome he was, how he reminded her of her first husband, and how lucky Olivia was to have found him and why on earth didn't she follow him to wherever it was he went?

Aunt Alyce never knew Jack hadn't wanted her to go with him. She didn't know Jack was hell-bent on being the next Indiana Jones, down to the hat and the attitude. What would Aunt Alyce say if she knew Jack was here with her on the very same island where they'd met?

She'd be incredulous to learn Olivia was going to choose a cottage by herself over a tent with Jack. That she was playing it safe rather than taking a chance with the man who'd get her aunt's vote for someone she'd most like to be marooned with on a desert island. Olivia knew exactly what she'd say if she were here.

"Don't be a fool, girl. Go. Go with him. Share that tent. Use your charm to get him back. It's fate. Fate brought you together. This is your last chance. Don't turn your back on him. He needs you and you need him."

Which just went to prove that age and wisdom didn't necessarily go together. An old tomb had brought them together, not fate. And Jack didn't need anybody. He'd never been so successful and so happy as he'd been after they'd separated. How did she know? Mutual friends had assured her Jack was getting along famously. They'd described parties he'd been to, honors he'd gotten and new friends he'd made. More power to him, she thought bitterly.

"You've got the clothes and I've got our tent and the sleeping bags," Jack said. "Jeep's outside and we've got a date with Alexander the Great and his followers." He loaded her bags in his arms and nodded at the door. He was like a racehorse at the starting gate. "Let's go."

"*Our* tent?" Warning bells went off in her head. Thank God for that empty cottage with her name on it. "No, Jack, I can't. I'm staying here in town. It's better that way."

"Okay, *your* tent," he said, brushing her words aside as if they were nothing but cobwebs. "It seems the rest are all spoken for, so I'll sleep outside. That way I won't hear you snoring."

"I don't snore."

"Look, Olivia, either we do this or we don't. If you can't handle a summer working with me 24/7 just say so. If you've got some hang-up, some residual feelings that make it impossible for you to stay at the site with me, tell me now. Yes or no. I thought we could do this without getting all emotional. Now, are we on or aren't we?"

He reached down and put on the wide-brimmed hat she'd bought him, giving her a jolt like an electrical current. He really looked like Indiana Jones, sexy, rugged and macho, like he could conquer the world. Let him conquer the world as long as he didn't conquer her.

She asked herself why she'd bought him that hat. It was because she knew how he'd look in it, and she couldn't resist. Well, she'd better develop some hard-core resistance and fast.

Olivia wracked her brain, desperately trying to think of a reason to say no to staying on-site aside from her fear of making the huge mistake of falling for Jack again. Even in his ridiculous borrowed clothes she'd had trouble keeping her head straight. Now in his new prefaded jeans molded to his legs and that hat, he was more dangerous than ever to the shield she'd put up around her heart. He stood there looking buff, tanned, eager to go, exuding an easy confidence in the face of opposition. He always had. He always would.

He was confident they'd find the lost tomb. Confident he'd pull the group together. Confident he'd survive whatever disaster came his way. Confident she'd come with him. Or was he? Wasn't there just a flicker of uncertainty in those dark-blue eyes that were looking at her so intently?

She took a deep breath and gave up. "No feelings," she said briskly. "We're on."

Jack nodded and reached for her hand. Instead of shaking it, he held it for a long moment and looked deep into her eyes. So deep he could see into her soul. He probably knew exactly what effect he had on her. "You won't regret it," he said. "I promise."

Once upon a time he promised to love her forever. So much for his promises.

CHAPTER FOUR

JUST like last time, seven years ago, the rented Jeep was full of equipment, shovels, picks, maps, augers, corers, a generator, gasoline, jugs of fresh water and a large picnic basket the hotel had packed for them at Jack's request.

Jack wanted to get this expedition off on the right foot. There were going to be hard times, both bad days and good. Crazy times with tempers flaring as things didn't go as planned, a heat wave, rain or any other kind of delay. He had a huge job ahead of him, and the hardest part was to convince Olivia they had a chance together. How he was going to do that without bringing up the painful past, he didn't know.

He didn't know how she felt about him now. He only knew that although the divorce was in the works, he had to give their marriage one last try. If she turned him down again, if it didn't work out, he didn't want to live the rest of his life knowing he hadn't given it his all.

The temperature was climbing. He'd hoped to get an early start to avoid the heat. But preparations got in the way. So he ordered lunch to go and he pictured a picnic under the trees overlooking the sea for just the two of them. To get this summer off to a good start. A second start. To forget the ferry incident and make it like old times. But he was smart enough to know old times were gone for good.

He just wanted a little time alone with her before the work started. It was almost too late for that. The workers had been preparing the site for the past week. The first group meeting was scheduled for later today, and the dig would really get underway tomorrow.

The road to the site was the same—rutted and winding. But this time there was more inside the Jeep than just equipment and supplies. There was tension that seemed to mount the closer they got to the site.

Jack felt it, but pretended it didn't exist. He warned himself not to expect too much. Either from Olivia or from the dig. Despite his easy assurances about how they could work together, no problem etc. etc., he was just as worried as Olivia might be about how they'd keep their distance during this long, hot summer. Especially since she insisted they present a united front. He told himself to relax and let nature take its course.

Hell, he didn't know if he could present a front like the one she wanted. He didn't want to keep his distance. He sure hadn't last night. He sure hadn't this morning when he saw her in her nightgown and his heart rate went through the roof. Then she appeared in those shorts, on anyone else an ordinary digging outfit, but her legs were anything but ordinary, long and smooth and unforgettable. As if he weren't in enough trouble as it was, now he was subjected to nonstop views of Olivia in a shirt that hugged her breasts and her gorgeous legs only inches away from him in the Jeep.

How in God's name was he going to keep any distance if they were sharing a tent? Because they weren't. He promised her he'd sleep outside.

And if it rained? Only a heartless wench would keep a man outside in the rain. Olivia was anything but heartless. If anything she felt too much, cared too much. Watching her try and fail to get pregnant was something he never wanted to go through again. Not that he'd ever have the chance to watch her go through anything again if he couldn't break down the barriers between them. This was clearly the end of the line for them. Unless… unless a miracle happened.

He saw the look on her face when she ran into him on the ferry. He saw dismay mixed with surprise. She was not exactly overjoyed to see him again. Maybe he should have told her in advance. No, she wouldn't have come. So this was their last hurrah. He told himself to make the best of it.

He scanned the sky for a glimpse of a dark cloud somewhere. Just a chance of rain. Nothing. "Looks like good weather," he said. Yep, he was going to be sleeping under the stars, or more likely tossing and turning under the stars, and she was going to be inside the tent sleeping soundly, dreaming of finding precious coins or pots instead of him.

"Beautiful," she agreed. "What is it about the afternoon sun in Greece that makes it brighter and warmer than anywhere else in the world? Maybe it's because of the white-washed buildings or the golden sand on the beaches."

"Or maybe it's me. Maybe I send good vibes out into the stratosphere."

She turned to look at him, her eyes narrowed, not a hint of a smile on her lips. "Why didn't I think of that? Of course it's you, Jack. The sun and the stars revolve around you. As well as the whole international world of archaeology. How could I forget?"

The wind had blown her sun-kissed blond hair across her cheek, and he had to grip the steering wheel hard to keep from reaching over and tucking the strands behind her ear. He wanted so much to run his hand through her silky hair and bury his face in it. But all he could do was look, and take his fill, because this might be his last chance.

He couldn't get his mind off that lacy bra she bought this morning. He told himself she hadn't bought it with him in mind, but he kept picturing how she'd look in it. For his own sanity, he had to concentrate on the work ahead. But he wasn't made of stone, was he?

The Jeep hit a bump in the road, and both he and Olivia bounced up and down. Her eyes widened.

"They haven't done much to this road," she said.

"Be glad we won't have to drive it every day," he said as they passed a group of men walking along wearing baggy black pants and stiff cotton overshirts. "In case you're having second thoughts about staying out here."

"No," she said. But she didn't sound completely sure. "What about the food?"

"Robbins hired a local cook for us as well as a crew to do the heavy digging and watchmen to guard the site. Everything ought to be in place by tonight. Including the computers, the generator and cameras. I know some people thought he was too old for this kind of dig, but he's very well organized. Thought of everything, so even though we lost all our personal stuff, it won't stop us from working. Robbins expects a lot from this summer, and he's spared no expense, using his grant money to do whatever it takes to make things go as smoothly as possible. If he wants to stay at the hotel and go off sightseeing some days, I won't complain. He's earned it. And it leaves us free to do the good stuff."

"Like finding that tomb."

He nodded. He loved seeing her eyes light up like that. Sure, all archaeologists appreciated the discovery of a site. But some were armchair academics, content to sit back and let others do the scut work. Robbins and some of his students were happiest back in the lab, or under the big tent looking at samples under a microscope.

Not Olivia. She'd be out there in the noonday sun knee-deep in dirt, sifting soil through her fingers, searching for shards of pottery with almost a second sense of where to find them.

"Anyone else staying out there overnight?" she asked. Her voice was level with just a slight undercurrent of something, maybe anxiety. Did she want company? Was she still nervous about being there with just him and one tent? Or was she looking forward to the solitude, as he was, once the sun went down, a late communal dinner was served outside and the others left to go back to town?

It could be awkward. Or it could be…something else. An opportunity to close the gap between him and the only woman he'd ever loved. If they didn't get back together, at least he wanted to set matters right before they parted for good at the end of the summer. That was all he asked. All he really expected.

He couldn't go on like this. Being married but not being together. It didn't work. Not for him and not for her. That's why she'd filed for divorce. He wondered when she was going to mention it. He sure wasn't going to.

"I don't know if anyone else will stay on-site," he said as if it didn't matter to him one way or another. But it did. He remembered those nights when they'd lie together under the stars, just the two of them, talking, or just looking at the sky, so much in tune with each other's thoughts that words weren't necessary. "The students will rent mopeds and go back and forth every day. They won't want to miss the nightlife in town, such as it is. You remember what that was like."

"No, actually I don't. You probably don't remember, but I was such a nerd I stayed up half the night poring over journals and maps, or trying to piece together bits and pieces of old pots." She smiled ruefully. "Not like you, playboy of the western world. I never understood how you could party all night and be up at dawn with a pick in your hands."

"I had a lot of energy to burn off."

"You still have a lot of energy," she said. "You swam from a sinking ship yesterday."

"Back then I was out looking for something, I don't even know what." But he knew. He was looking for her, before he even knew she existed. He'd be out drinking and dancing the *Ziebekiko* all night, flirting, laughing, being the life of the party, knowing something was missing from his life. But what? Or whom?

He didn't know what was missing until he saw her, really saw her one day when she uncovered the pieces of a small statue of Zeus. He took a picture of her, kept it on his desk. Even without it, he'd never forget the look on her face of wonder and delight.

"I thought I was Zorba the Greek," he said.

"I thought you were, too," she said. He couldn't see her face; she was looking out the side window. But her voice held a note of sadness.

"I didn't know you noticed," he said.

"Everyone noticed you."

"What else could I do but go out on the town? I hadn't met you yet."

"You'd met me. You didn't notice me."

"How could I? You were covered with dust."

She laughed. There was nothing like her laughter. It was like uncorking a bottle of champagne, all bubbles and effervescence and intoxicating even before you'd tasted a drop. A man could get drunk on her laughter. Or even addicted to it if he wasn't careful. He wanted to hear her laugh again. It had been so long. Much too long.

"You've always been a partyer," she said.

"Not always." Only when she wasn't around. Then he felt restless, unable to relax. When he first went to Cal he'd gone out all the time with colleagues, hanging out at the campus hot spots, dining with colleagues, never alone. But that got old fast.

"Let's not talk about the past, okay?" she said.

He was all for that. But sometime they'd have to talk about the past because without it, they couldn't move forward.

"Tell me why you think this tomb could be Alexander's," she asked.

"Alexander? Probably not. But someone else important. Or they wouldn't have gone to all that trouble to hide it with decoys and false entrances."

"What about his wife or his son or maybe the leader of his footguards. They've never found his tomb, have they?" she asked.

With the conversation switched to safer subjects, she leaned back and seemed to relax.

"Everyone is sure Alexander's buried at Memphis in Egypt," he said. "Except me."

"You still think his tomb is in Alexandria, do you?" she asked.

"If it's true his body was smuggled there from Babylon where he died, then that's where it should be. He founded the city. It's named after him. It was the center of learning, the greatest library of the ancient world."

"Maybe you just want him to be there," Olivia suggested. "Because it's right that he should be."

"You think I'd let my judgment be colored by what I want to believe?"

"What you want to believe is often what really happened. You have good instincts. You're usually right about these things."

"Why, Olivia," he said with mock surprise. "Is that a compliment?"

"You don't need praise from me, Jack. You've got your students convinced you're a superhero. You're Mr. Archaeology. You should have heard them last night. They weren't even worried you'd make it to shore."

"Were you?"

"I was more than worried. I was furious. All I could think of was the time you insisted on climbing that cliff in the Olduvai Gorge to pry off that fossil. You fell twelve feet and you were unconscious."

"For a few minutes, sure. But the fossil was intact. And my head is as good as new."

"That's debatable," she said. "The next day you lowered yourself into a cave between the rocks and got stuck there. Why? Because you wanted to see if there were paintings on the wall."

"There were."

"There weren't."

"Well, maybe not paintings. They were more drawings."

"Scratches."

"If you don't take chances, Olivia, you never find what you're looking for."

"If you don't take extreme chances, you might live to see old age."

"The value of old age is greatly exaggerated. Except for your aunt of course. You'll probably be just like her when you're eighty-eight."

"Eighty-nine," she said. "I doubt it. That's the kind of wife you should have had, a wild, crazy, dance-till-dawn chance-taker."

"That's not true," he said, suddenly serious.

Warning bells sounded. They said, "Don't let the conversation get too real."

"Anyway the students think you're the greatest," she said lightly.

"But not as great as Alexander," he said.

"No one's as great as he was. That's why his empire fell apart after he died."

"And his wife had to hit the road with their son," he said. "The son he never saw."

Olivia studied Jack's hands on the wheel. She'd fallen in love with his hands. Long, strong and so capable. Capable of scraping centuries of dirt from a statue or riffling the pages of a book or tenderly smoothing away a tear from her cheek.

She supposed he might be thinking it was a tragedy that Alexander never knew his son. But Jack's eyes were on the road. His expression revealed nothing.

"Of course I'd love to find her tomb someday. So would every other archaeologist," she said.

"That's why you're here, isn't it?" he asked, his

eyes narrowed, a half smile on his face. "To track down Roxane."

"She's one of the most interesting characters of the era. But I couldn't get that lucky. I'll be happy if we uncover the tomb at last and find a few coins or a glass bowl."

"I read your article on Alexander's wife."

"What did you think of it?"

"Fascinating."

"Really?" she said with surprise. "That's the nicest thing you've said to me since we got here. Be careful, I might get carried away." Jack wasn't someone who'd toss empty compliments her way.

"Don't tell me you don't get plenty of strokes. I saw where you won the Professor of the Year Award the students give. They're a choosy bunch."

"I was happy about that. I love my students. At least the ones who stay awake in class."

"What more have you learned about the beautiful Roxane?" he asked.

"Nothing new. Just the shocking stuff that makes a good story. She had his second wife killed, and she went to live with his mother after he died. I'll tell you what I don't know, and that's where she's buried."

"I hope you won't be disappointed if this isn't it."

"No, not at all. I just hope we can find the tomb. Anybody's tomb. That no one else has gotten to it before us."

"Whoever it is doesn't much matter," he added, "if it fills in some gaps in what we know about the period. That's why I wanted you along."

"To fill in the gaps," she said. Of course. Why else would he want her? Nothing personal. Nothing to do with those divorce papers. When was he ever going to mention them? Was he waiting for her to bring it up?

"No one knows Hellenistic tombs like you do," he said.

Olivia should have felt good. She should be proud he wanted her along for her knowledge of the period. But she wasn't. Instead she felt deflated, as if he'd punctured her balloon. It was her own fault. She'd allowed herself to think he wanted her there because he realized he couldn't live without her, that he wanted to spend the summer with her and had arranged it so that it happened. He'd made it clear that wasn't the case. She wrapped her arms across her waist. About time for a reality check.

"*I've* never gotten Professor of the Year. I never will," he said.

"What do you mean? It's just a matter of time. Your students adore you. Isn't that enough?"

He turned to give her a sharp look. "No, it's not," he said. "I'll never be the teacher you are. You know why. I haven't got your patience or your perseverance. You know my faults better than anyone."

Yes, she did. She had to keep reminding herself of them, his pride that sometimes bordered on arrogance. He was a little too sure of himself. He bowled over anyone or anything who got in his way. To be fair, he was not only brilliant, he worked hard and he inspired admiration from friends and enemies alike. He was ambitious, and he used his students to further his research. But he always gave them credit. He was a dynamic lecturer and a fair grader. Not loving her anymore didn't constitute a fault, just a fact she'd better get used to.

"We were discussing Alexander and his wife," she said. "Why do all our conversations always turn personal?" She didn't really want an answer to that one. "I'd be glad to list Alexander's faults. Vengeful and militaristic, but brilliant and charismatic, too. Oh, look, here's the road." Fortunately the discussion was over.

"We're with the archaeology team." Jack showed his ID card to the guard, and he waved them through a wide wooden gate.

"That's new," Olivia murmured. As they drove past the farmer's fields planted with golden wheat waving in the sun, past sheep grazing on green grass, she remembered the first time she'd been there and how excited she'd been as they neared the site of the ancient tomb.

Now she was older, wiser and more jaded. There had been other tombs, other digs. There was more at stake now and she had more to lose. Like Jack. As if she hadn't already lost him two years ago.

She knew what she wanted now. But only in terms of pottery and artifacts. In terms of life? That was a harder question. Before she could come up with any answers for herself, they came to another gate with another guard.

"More security this time," Jack muttered. "Hope it's overkill. Hope we don't need it." Again he showed his card and they parked inside the gate in a grove of olive trees.

"You think locals could be out to rob the tomb?" she asked, stepping out of the Jeep with a glance over her shoulder. The scene was so peaceful, so tranquil, so pastoral, she couldn't believe they had anything to worry about.

"Or a team from another school. Robbins tried to keep it quiet that we'd gotten permission to come back again this year, but word may have leaked out. You know how archaeologists are."

"Greedy, territorial and passionate. Is that what you mean?"

He grinned at her from the other side of the Jeep. His eyes narrowed and laugh lines appeared at the corners. "I'll only admit to the passionate part."

He'd done it again, sent her pulse racing with just a look, just an offhand remark. Jack, passionate? Oh, yes. He used to say that together they made the gods jealous. It all came back to her, the same helpless feeling of being swept away by his sheer magnetism.

He lifted the picnic basket out of the back. "Let's eat before we do anything else. I didn't have lunch. Contrary to popular opinion, I'm not a superhero and I need some food before I unload our stuff. I suspect dinner won't be until late, Greek time."

"What about the others? Aren't we all going to eat together?" she asked nervously. She didn't want a romantic picnic for two. That was a bad way to start off the dig.

"I don't see any others, do you?" he asked. "Come on, let's eat."

She could hardly refuse without seeming like she was paranoid. What could happen at a picnic in full daylight even if no one else was around?

They walked across the field with the old excavation still there, marked off with rocks and occasional wooden posts. They skirted a large, shallow, open pit and stopped to gaze down at the rough-hewn rocks, the marked-off lines of a long-ago, forgotten community complete with a temple and a burial site.

"The tomb is down there. I know it is," she said softly.

"If it is we'll find it. We've got a better crew, more equipment and good people. We'll find it this time. We have to."

She nodded. If sheer willpower would do it, they would find it. Jack had enough of that. There was a buzz in the air. Men in overalls were working everywhere, not just with picks and shovels at the excavation, but also setting up a huge open-air tent and tables under it.

"Everything's bigger and better this year," she noted.

"Yeah, over there's the portable toilets and a shower. Cold water, but last time we had no showers, just the sea below on the beach. Glad you came?"

"Of course." What did he expect her to say? She *was* glad she'd come. For now. It was her favorite time. With a whole summer ahead of her. Anything could happen. It was the most exciting time to be here. The beginning of a dig. The first day on the site. It was broad daylight; more people would be arriving soon. No reason to be afraid of getting too close to Jack. Jack wasn't the problem. She was. All she needed was an extra dose of willpower. If only it came in tablets at the local pharmacy.

She also had to keep her guard up. He wasn't there to seduce her. The worst he could do was try to convince her to get back together. She doubted he would try. Just looking at him, seeing him bounce back after an ordeal at sea, was enough to tell her he was doing just fine without her. Jack didn't need anyone. He was the consummate independent.

As if on autopilot, without even discussing it, they headed toward a grove of pine trees on the cliff. Maybe he didn't remember it was once their favorite spot to watch the sun go down into the Aegean. Maybe he didn't remember they'd bought a wide-striped hammock in town and hung it between two trees. A hammock big enough for two. A hammock she still had stashed away in a closet at home. She needed to get rid of it, to stop clinging to the past. If only she didn't have such a good memory, it would make things so much easier.

She opened their basket and spread a large checkered tablecloth on the grass. Jack pulled out a bottle of red country wine and opened it. He poured some into two paper cups and handed her one.

"Here's to a great summer," he said, raising his cup. He didn't say *our last*, but she knew it was.

"Here's to finding the tomb," she said. *Keep it light. Keep it impersonal.*

"Here's to finding everything we're looking for," he said. He held her gaze for a long moment while she considered what he meant by that.

Then she took a sip of wine, looked away and pretended she hadn't even heard that last remark. Of course he just meant artifacts and old bones, but he could have meant something else.

"Have you ever found everything you were looking for on a dig?" she asked.

"Just once," he said. He shot a look in her direction, his gaze so intense he could only mean one thing. The last time they were here, they'd found each other.

"I try not to get my hopes up," she said, shading her eyes and looking out to sea to avoid his gaze. "Sometimes I find what I'm looking for, sometimes it's something else entirely. Sometimes the tomb's empty. Sometimes the pottery has turned to dust. It's all part of the game."

"You're philosophical today," he remarked.

"It's the only way to be," she said, keeping her eyes on the white sail of a small boat floating in a cobalt sea. "Otherwise you're setting yourself up for disappointment." She realized she sounded like a know-it-all, but that was better than playing the dangerous game of Memories.

She sat down on a flat rock and busily started unloading the picnic basket. First a loaf of crusty bread, then a small bottle of fruity, fragrant olive oil. She sniffed it and sighed with pleasure.

"Now I know we're back in Greece," she said.

He sat on the edge of the tablecloth across from her, leaned forward and broke off a piece of bread. "You know the folk tale about the stubborn and rebellious Greek wife, don't you?"

"No, but I have a feeling you're going to tell me," she said, opening a container of fava beans and one of tiny, cold, marinated artichokes. Folk tales were a better topic than talking about themselves and the past.

"She refused to submit to her husband. So for seven

days and seven nights he rubbed her body with olive oil. By the eighth day, she gave in and they made love under the olive trees."

"Since it's a folk tale, I suppose they lived happily ever after?" she said, handing him the olive oil.

"Of course."

Olivia kept busy opening containers, one after another of delicious Greek specialties. It was a good distraction. The look in his eyes told her what she didn't want to admit. *There's no subject, no folk tale, nothing that doesn't relate to us and our situation. Whether it's about marriage, sex, the past or the future. It's all about us.*

"Here, try this," she said, handing him a paper plate with sliced cucumber, tiny tomatoes bursting with flavor and a slab of white feta cheese.

"*Horiatiki salata*, my favorite," he said. "That brings back memories."

"What doesn't?" she muttered.

Memories were threatening to take over the present. What was she going to do about it?

CHAPTER FIVE

"HELLO, lady."

Olivia opened her eyes. After lunch she must have drifted off to sleep while reclining on the linen cloth under the trees.

She sat up. "Elias, what are you doing here?"

"My father, he works here." He pointed across the field to the men unloading equipment from a flatbed truck.

Olivia was relieved to know he had at least one parent. Still, she couldn't resist offering him something to eat. He always looked hungry, but maybe that was just her imagination, just her need to nurture coming out. Someone had repacked the picnic basket. Someone who must have been Jack. Jack was the one who should be napping under the trees, not her. He'd slept in a chair all night, while she'd had the bed.

She found a bunch of purple grapes in the basket, handed them to Elias who promptly popped them into his mouth. She smiled at the sight of grape juice dribbling down his chin and refrained from mopping it up with a napkin. At his age he probably wouldn't appreciate it.

"How old are you Elias?"

"Nine."

"Where do you live?" she asked, when what she really wanted to know was, *How do you live and who takes care of you?*

The boy pointed off in the distance and Olivia had to be content with that. She had no business prying into anyone's life.

She looked around and saw Jack and Dr. Robbins talking earnestly near the excavation. A few students were wandering around. She hoped they hadn't seen her sleeping. Jack should have woken her up. She ran her hand through her hair. The sun was low in the sky, turning the hills in the distance behind them to gold. The sea was smooth as glass. All this beauty and a summer of discovery ahead of her. She mustn't let anything like the messy situation with Jack spoil it.

She stood, folded the cloth and put it in the basket.

"Come," she said to Elias, "I want you to meet my—" She stopped. "Someone," she finished lamely.

Jack met her halfway across the field. "Who's this?" he asked. "Friend of yours?"

"This is Elias. He helped me carry my bags this morning. It turns out his father is one of the workers."

Elias nodded and pointed to one of the men in black pants and a white shirt.

"Want a job?" Jack asked him.

His eyes widened, and he grinned broadly.

"We need someone small to climb down and attach a rope for us."

Olivia frowned. "Is it dangerous?"

"No. Come on, I'll show you."

When she saw Jack only wanted Elias to jump a few feet down into the excavation to reach into a tunnel and tie a rope to a hook, and would pay him to do it, Olivia went to greet Marilyn and some of the students from Jack's university.

"What a spot," a girl named Sandy said. "This is beautiful. I hear you've been here before, Mrs...."

"Call me Olivia," Olivia said. She glanced at Marilyn. She hoped she wasn't telling everyone her marital status and her history. Naturally anyone from Jack's school would be curious about her. She could just hear the unspoken questions that hung in the air.

Why don't you live together?

Are you getting a divorce?

Or are you getting back together again?

Where did you meet?

When did you split up?

Why? Why? Why?

"Tell us about it," an owlish girl named Jenny with big glasses and her hair in a ponytail said.

"First we're lucky to be here," Olivia said.

"The site has been closed for years," Marilyn explained to the three girls clustered around them.

"So we don't know what state the ruins are in," Olivia added. "I understand that when the farm changed hands after we left the last time, the new owner closed the road and the property. Afraid of tomb robbers, gold diggers, or whatever. He didn't see the potential value of the excavation. To him it was just a nuisance."

"But now it's been taken over by the local government, which realizes the potential of the site," Marilyn added.

"That's right. Apparently they want to encourage tourism. Maybe have a museum in town, if we find something important," Olivia said. "They were allowed to do a lot of prep work on the site before we got here. So we can make some good progress." She'd learned a lot in the briefing she'd gotten before she left. She should have guessed at the time that Jack was a part of it. She should have recognized his hand in it. His name was written all over it.

"Is it true we only have this summer to do it?" the girl asked.

Olivia nodded. "I'm afraid so. It's a one-year lease."

"But who knows?" Marilyn said. "If we find something important…" They all hoped for something big. If they found an important tomb here, if there were valuable artifacts, it could lead to more digs, an extended lease… Other summers. Other summers without her. She'd come this year without knowing Jack would be here. She would make other plans for next summer and the ones after that. She would make sure he wasn't a part of them.

"I read your article on Alexander's wife," Sandy said to Olivia when the others wandered off to inspect the tables under the tent. "I thought it was amazing."

Olivia blushed with pleasure. "I'm always surprised anyone reads those obscure journals."

"Dr. Oakley assigned it to us," Sandy said. "In his Archaeology 101 class. He said it was one of the best pieces he'd seen."

"Oh," Olivia said faintly.

"He's a great teacher," Sandy said. "I was lucky to get in. His classes fill up so fast. He inspired me. Now I want to be an archaeologist like you."

"Me? I'm not sure…"

"Especially when I saw that picture of you on the desk in his office. When you discovered that little statue. That was awesome."

Olivia rocked back on her heels. Jack had a picture of her on his desk? She didn't have one of him anywhere she could see it. She'd packed them all away in a box in her closet. It hurt too much to see that photo of him standing at the edge of an excavation, holding an amphora in his hand, smiling at the camera, smiling at her, reminding her of happier times. Obviously, looking at her photo every day meant nothing to him, he probably had all kinds of pictures on his desk of other people and other artifacts. They'd just become part of the furniture.

"There you are," Jack said, coming up behind her with Elias at his side. "We're going down to the beach to see if the old dock is still there so we could launch a boat from here. I see you've met Sandy."

Sandy nodded enthusiastically. "I was just telling your…Mrs.…Olivia, that I want to be an archaeologist like her someday."

Jack nodded. Who wouldn't want to be like Olivia?

She'd probably inspired dozens of other young women to go into the field. Anyone could see why. She was brainy and beautiful. She was modest but full of confidence, too. And she had an enthusiasm for the field that was contagious.

"Why not?" he said. It was a worthwhile goal, but no one would ever be like Olivia, no matter how hard they tried, how hard they studied. She was one of a kind and he'd been a fool to ever let her go. Or rather he'd been a fool to leave her.

If he'd known then what he knew now, he wouldn't have gone. He'd gained prestige, salary and authority, but he'd lost her. It was too late now to change anything or to take back the hurtful words they'd exchanged. Way, way too late. He could only make the best of this summer and then make the best of the rest of his life. He had no other choice.

"Come down to the beach," he said. "I want to show you something."

"Just us?" she said, looking around for company. "I don't want people to think…"

"Then bring your friend."

He and Olivia clambered down the steep path together with Elias skipping and sliding ahead of them, apparently fearless.

"Cute kid," he said.

"I know. This morning I thought he was alone in the world, begging tourists for loose change. I had this crazy desire to take him under my wing, but now I find out he has a father. I'm relieved."

He glanced at Olivia, wondering if she really was relieved or a little disappointed. Maybe she still longed for a child to take care of. He wouldn't know how she felt about motherhood at this point, and he sure wasn't going to ask. He'd long ago given up hope of their having a baby. And he'd almost given up hope of their getting back together.

The more he thought about it the more he realized it was wrong to think a reconciliation was possible. If he didn't know it before, he knew it now. She'd made it very clear it was over. She wouldn't have even come on this trip if she'd known he was part of it.

She stumbled over a loose rock. He turned, grabbed her hand and didn't let go. He wondered if she had ever considered adoption when she hadn't gotten pregnant. Is that what she wanted now since she couldn't have her own baby? He thought she'd put it out of her mind, but *he* hadn't, so why should she?

The beach was wide and sandy. The water was calm and warm. The old dock they'd come to look at was falling apart.

"What did you want to show me?" she asked.

"The dock. It needs work," Jack said, testing the boards. "Before we can bring a boat here."

"We didn't have one last time," she said. "Why do we need one?"

"We might want to visit some other islands this time." He pointed to a dark shape on the horizon. "Like Antihyphasis, where there's supposed to be a well-preserved temple to Artemis."

"I'd like to see that," she said.

"Thought you would." He wanted to take her everywhere she wanted to go. Besides work there had to be time off. He wanted to make it a summer she'd never forget. To make every minute meaningful. Because that's all they'd have, this one last summer to make new memories. To erase the painful ones in the past. "We'll get the workers down here. Then bring a small boat and tie it up."

Olivia took her shoes off and let the warm clear water lap at her ankles. The wet sand oozed through her toes, and she sighed with pure sensual pleasure. Elias was tossing stones out into the water.

"Bring your suit?" Jack asked her.

"I brought one, but it went down with my suitcase. I'll have to buy another one in town."

"Last time…"

"Jack," she said, shooting a warning glance in his direction. She knew what he was going to say. *Last time we didn't wear suits. We swam nude at night after everyone else had retired.* "This isn't last time."

"I'm aware of that," he said. "I'm also aware that we're still married. For now. Which means something."

"Which means nothing. Except a formality."

"If that's all it is, then we ought to end it," he said. Might as well bring it up now as later.

The sea was calm, but Olivia felt shock waves hit her like a tidal wave.

"Is that what you want?" she asked, blinking rapidly to keep back the sudden tears.

"I'm not the one who filed the papers," he said. "We either get divorced or you join me at Cal U."

"It's not that easy," she said.

"Nothing worthwhile is easy." He gave her a long look full of meaning. The meaning she knew only too well. Another time he might have stalked across the sand and swept her into his arms and kissed her hard and deep until they were both swept up by a fiery desire they couldn't resist.

Of course, he did nothing like that. He just continued to give her a look full of smoldering passion. That made her shake inside. His lips might say he wanted a divorce, but his eyes said he wanted to make love to her.

What else could he do but look? They weren't alone and she hadn't kissed him or barely touched him for the past two years. She had no intention of starting now. In fact, she shouldn't have come down to the beach with him.

"Is this really a good time to discuss this?" she asked with a glance at Elias still tossing stones from the edge of the water. She didn't want to discuss it at all, anytime.

The least-painful way to end this marriage would be at the end of the summer by mail. No tears, no recriminations, no regrets. Just a simple document. All he had to do was sign it. Then she'd sign it and it would all be over. Seven years of marriage. The last two being separated, so they didn't really count. It sounded so simple. But it wasn't. For him maybe, but not for her.

"Elias, let me show you how to skip stones," Jack said, flipping his attention from Olivia to the boy on the sand. Jack reached down for a handful of flat, polished stones.

There he went again, changing the subject, or creating a diversion to escape an awkward situation. Being physically close to him was too hard. Even in the heat of the day she felt a little chill run up her spine when he gave her that look she once knew so well. A look that said he wanted her and he knew she wanted him. Here on an idyllic beach in Greece with Jack playing the Indiana Jones character where everything he said had a double or triple meaning, she couldn't think straight.

As she watched him show Elias how to skip stones and heard the boy's excited shouts when he mastered the art of multiple skipping, she felt an old familiar twinge of regret. Regret for not giving Jack the son he wanted.

She'd tried, God knew she'd tried, but maybe not hard enough, not long enough. If they'd be able to have a baby, they might still be together.

"Jack. Olivia." Someone was calling from the top of the cliff.

She turned and looked up. It was Dr. Robbins's assistant. She was waving.

"We'd better go back," she called to Jack. "We're being paged. I have a feeling we're getting under way."

Her stomach churned. No more stalling. No possibility of backing out of the expedition. This was it. Time to get serious. The clock was ticking. One more summer. One more time. One last chance to dig with Jack.

A chance to fill the days with digging and piecing together old objects. Separately. And the nights? No problem. After a late dinner at the long tables under the tent with the whole team, let the students take off for town and the tavernas and clubs. Then for those who were left on the site, *Please let it be more than just she and Jack*, they'd be so tired after a day of hard work, they'd retire to their tents and promptly fall asleep. At least, that was the plan. And she intended to stick to it.

After a lengthy meeting where Dr. Robbins handed out walkie-talkies, presented the group with several computers to be set up on tables in another tent and handed out work sheets and digital cameras to record their finds, Jack gave an inspiring pep talk.

Olivia stood at the edge of the group, leaning against a cedar tree, listening to Jack talk about goals and expectations. Now there was a topic he was good at, except when it came to them. Except when it got personal.

He took off his Indiana Jones hat and talked about the age of Alexander the Great and what they might find here on this spot. He spoke about the good fortune of having the unexpected opportunity to dig here again one last time. How important this site was to their knowledge of the Hellenistic era. He told them not to have too many unrealistic hopes or take anything for granted.

He could have been talking to her. In fact, she felt his eyes on her the whole time. Everything he said about unrealistic hopes could have applied to them, too. But it didn't. Jack was the last person to air their problems in public or even private.

She'd forgotten just how dynamic a speaker he was. How inspiring. He was so enthusiastic it was no wonder the students fought to get into his classes. She wouldn't be surprised if the girls lined up outside his office to talk to him about their research papers or just to get near him.

That shouldn't bother her so much. If their marriage was over, he should find someone else. Life was too short to spend it alone. At least, that's what Aunt Alyce would say. Not that she was in favor of a divorce for her favorite great-niece. The only divorce she favored was her own some sixty years ago, which left her free to cavort with many other men over the years, some a fraction of her age.

Jack was the most loyal husband a woman could want, Aunt Alyce pointed out. As far as Olivia knew he still honored his marriage vows because they were still legally married. As did she. But how many men separated from their wives, six hundred miles apart, would do that?

Maybe he hadn't. She looked around at the crowd of young students, at the attractive girls gazing dreamy-eyed at Jack. Did they talk about him after class? Did they refer to him as Professor McDreamy? What if they did? She had no more rights to him.

Maybe that's why he'd practically threatened her. Either join him at Cal U or…*get divorced*. Did he mean it? Yes, he did.

The group then divided up into small teams. She and Jack were on the same team. That was a mistake. She had to get herself reassigned. There were individual meetings held under trees or at picnic tables. Olivia couldn't concentrate on the details of the work their team was assigned to do.

She kept glancing over her shoulder at the sun setting into the sea. What was wrong with her? She had a wild desire to run back down to the beach and float in the azure sea, letting the water caress her body. She was acting like a hopeless romantic on a vacation and not a dig.

After dark someone started the generator, and the strings of incandescent bulbs strung around the outside of the tents lit up giving the whole area a fairy-land atmosphere. Now she was even more adrift, more removed from the task at hand.

The air was filled with the smell of savory lamb cooking on a spit. The cook's assistants had covered the tables in the main tent with locally hand-woven cloths, bottles of spring water, ouzo and a local red wine.

"You okay?" Jack asked when the last meeting broke up. He caught her outside the tent, tilted her chin with his thumb for a better look, and frowned at her.

She swallowed hard. That concerned look in his eyes could melt her resolve faster than the noonday sun.

"Of course."

"You looked like you went AWOL there for a while."

"Sorry, I… You know, in the past few years I've had a lot of responsibility on the digs. This year is different. I'm just one of the group. Like being a grad assistant again. It's a funny feeling."

"Good or bad?"

"I'm not sure. I just feel different, like kicking back, having a good time instead of being responsible and knuckling down to do the hard work."

"You mean you want to go to town to the clubs at night?" He sounded surprised.

"No, no, not that." She looked down at her bare toes

in her sandals still coated with sand. "I don't know what I want to do. One thing I know is that I can't be on your team."

"Fine," he said, as if he didn't care one way or the other. "But think it over. You'll feel better after dinner. You didn't eat much for lunch."

"I won't change my mind," she said. Not unless she was crazy. She sniffed the air. "It smells great. Sure beats the food we had last time."

"When everyone took turns cooking. Some good, some not so good."

"You made a stew one night. It wasn't bad."

"Is that why you fell for me, my cooking?"

"Until I found out one dish was all you could make."

"Hey, don't knock it. It was my signature dish."

"Without it we would have starved."

"You still make that heirloom tomato spaghetti sauce?"

"I don't really cook at all anymore." Why bother cooking for one person? So much easier to open a can of soup or spread peanut butter on a piece of toast and call it dinner. How different from cooking for Jack on weekends when she had time, making his favorite dishes, working together in the kitchen when he invited his whole department for dinner at the last minute.

"I don't, either," he said flatly. "I live on takeout."

She glanced at his broad shoulders, flat stomach and muscular arms. Whatever he was eating didn't seem to have done him any harm. But she was surprised he wasn't inundated with dinner invitations from sympathetic female colleagues who felt sorry for him being on his own, or even students, though fraternizing with undergrad girls was frowned on.

She carefully chose a seat between Marilyn and one of Jack's students at dinner. Jack was at the far end of the table. From now on she was going to be extracareful to let everyone know they were definitely not a couple. They weren't together at all. Yes, they might work together, but that was all. They wouldn't eat together and they most definitely wouldn't sleep together.

Still, there were times when her gaze happened to meet his. At one point he lifted his wineglass to her in a silent toast. Second time today. She looked away, turning to her dinner companions in an effort to get him out of her line of sight and, even more important, out of her mind. As if she could.

"Staying out here?" Marilyn asked with a little smile as she cut into a flaky honey-drenched pastry. "With Jack?"

"No, not with Jack," Olivia said firmly. No matter what it looked like, she was *not* staying with Jack. Maybe she ought to make an announcement. "I'm not sure who is staying out here. What about you?"

"Back to the hotel for me. I'm too old to sleep on the ground. We'll be back early in the morning." Later, on her way to the van in the driveway, she called out loudly, "Be good now."

Olivia sighed loudly. What more could she say to quell the rumors? She could only hope no one knew who Marilyn was talking to. And she was glad it was too dark for anyone to see her blush.

As the last van pulled away and the last student on his moped, the generator shut down for the night and the lights went out. Good thing the moon had just dipped behind a cloud. And she had a flashlight.

"Guess it's just you and me." Jack appeared from the grove of cedar trees with his arms full.

"Oh, no, really?" Her heart fell. "Everyone else has left?"

"Yep," he said cheerfully. "Here's *your* tent," he said, handing her the stakes and her bags to carry.

"It doesn't seem fair," she said.

"Life isn't fair, Olivia," he said. "Some people get the big bed and the tent and some have to sleep on the cold hard ground."

"If you think you're going to make me feel guilty…"

"I don't. But if you have trouble sleeping…"

"I won't." Liar. She'd had trouble sleeping ever since Jack left. Until last night when she was under the same roof as him for the first time in two years. Coincidence or not? After he left for Cal U she'd tried hot milk, hot baths and over-the-counter sleeping pills. Nothing took the place of sleeping with the man she'd married. Now what would happen? Nothing, that's what.

CHAPTER SIX

OLIVIA was afraid the spot they'd picked for the tent was the same place as last time. In the dark she wasn't sure. She hoped not. She didn't need any more memories of their past late-night meetings, their secret trysts, hidden kisses and hushed whispers.

After they chose the spot in a grove of trees, Jack hung a gas lantern from the limb of a cypress tree and they worked together setting up the large tent, just like they used to do, pounding the stakes into the ground and arranging the rain guard carefully over the top. He tossed her bags inside along with their picnic basket and her sleeping bag and pillow, then he ducked inside and she followed. He stood in the center looking around, the top of his head brushing the nylon roof.

"I know what you're thinking," she said. "I want you to stop."

He raised his eyebrows.

"You're thinking the tent is big enough for two. It's not."

"Not me."

"We are not sharing. I don't care if it's as big as a

Ringling Brothers tent and you could fit a parade of elephants into it. We had an agreement."

"I never go back on my word," he said earnestly. "Good night, Olivia."

She had to admit she'd expected an argument from him. Or at least a protest. She was relieved he was calling it a day. She wanted him out of her tent and as far away as possible.

She was glad he didn't suggest a card game by the light of the lantern. She would never ever ask him to give her a back rub again the way he used to. That was a sure way to trouble. All she could think of was other digs, other summers where they shared their hopes, their dreams, a tent, a sleeping bag and just about everything else.

"Are the showers set up?" she asked.

"Not yet. But there's the beach. Oh, I forgot, you don't have your suit."

"Do you?"

"No, but I don't have an exaggerated sense of modesty."

"You have no modesty at all," she said. "But I bought us each a bathrobe from the hotel."

"Good girl, Olivia. Are you thinking what I'm thinking? We wear our robes to the beach, then leave them on the shore."

"You'll cover your eyes until I get into the water?"

"Of course."

Still, she hesitated. She'd vowed to keep her distance from him. But the water was so warm and it was so dark. What harm could it do to go for a swim? No one would know. She opened the package with the robes neatly folded inside and gave him one. He went outside and left her alone to undress. Finally alone, she had a funny little feeling in the pit of her stomach, a feeling of anticipation and a warning in her head that told her this was not her best idea.

Before she could change her mind, she quickly stripped down to her bare skin and wrapped the soft terry cloth robe around her. How could anything that felt so good be wrong?

Jack stood outside her tent, adrenaline pumping through his veins, sure he'd just won the lottery. Unless he was dreaming. He'd had this dream before. Olivia slipping out of her clothes. Olivia coming to him as beautiful as a mermaid in the sea. He and Olivia together again.

Or he could be overreacting. It was just a midnight swim. No big deal. No, it was a midnight swim with Olivia and it was a big deal. It was *her* idea. Not his. But it was the best idea he'd heard in days or weeks or months. Skinny-dipping with Olivia in the warm Aegean Sea.

Sure, he'd promised to cover his eyes, but she really didn't expect him to, did she?

He'd just undressed and stacked his clothes next to his sleeping bag about ten yards from her tent when she appeared in her robe that matched his, which he hadn't yet put on.

"Oh, you're not ready," she said, turning around with her back to him.

"Sorry, I was thinking…about the dig." He thrust his arms into the sleeves of the robe. If she believed that, he could probably sell her anything. "Ready," he said.

She looked like an illusion, with the moonlight turning her hair to silver and her white robe. A breathtaking illusion. He walked up and touched her, grazing one finger across her cheek.

"Just wanted to see if you were real."

She laughed breathlessly.

She was real. And beautiful. So real and so beautiful that his heart pounded so loudly in his chest he was afraid she'd hear it. But then, she'd heard it before.

"We could take a flashlight," he suggested.

"The moon's pretty bright," she said.

He reached for her hand so she wouldn't stumble; unless she stumbled into his arms like she had on the ferry. The next time, he didn't want it to be an accident. He wanted her to want him as much as he wanted her. He wanted to feel her arms around him, clinging to him. He wanted to hold her like he'd never let her go. To kiss her again until she melted in his arms.

He told himself it wasn't going to happen. It was too soon, too early. If she was going to come around, it would take all summer. Right now he couldn't wait. His heart was still pounding, telling him now, now, now. With her hand in his, the ribbon of moonlight on the water, anything was possible.

On the beach he kept his promise and turned away until he heard her splash into the water. He dropped his robe next to hers and plunged into the water until he was waist deep. Then he dove under and came up yards later to where she was.

He faced her, treading water, with his eyes on her face.

"This was a good idea," he said. Which was the understatement of the year. He would not, could not, look down at her breasts. But he knew how they'd look in the moonlight with the clear water rippling over her.

They swam together, straight out into the calm sea with sure steady strokes, until he turned over and floated on his back and looked up at the moon.

"We should do this every night," he said. "We used to."

Olivia looked up at the stars. "We used to do a lot of things that we won't be doing again."

He didn't say anything, but his silence spoke volumes.

She kicked her feet vigorously, watching the water spray in silver droplets. Looking back at the beach with their robes on the sand, then up at the outline of the cliff, she wished she could stay in the water forever.

Of course they could *not* do this every night. She shouldn't have come tonight. Swimming was fine, but it led to other dangers like making love under the stars. She wasn't going to do that this summer.

She was many things, but she was not a glutton for punishment. She'd learned her lesson. If she gave in to temptation, and Jack was temptation itself, she'd be setting herself up for a crash at the end of the summer. She'd recovered the last time they split up; she couldn't do it again. She had to be able to walk away from him in September with her pride and her ego intact. And go back to her old life, her old single life, just as he'd go back to his.

The water caressed her thighs, her arms, her breasts, making her skin tingle with awareness. She felt free and weightless. It was easy to tell herself what she had to do, but she wanted Jack with a fierce desire that coursed through her body. She'd forgotten she could feel that way, more alive and more aware than she was with anyone else.

She knew only too well what lovemaking would do to their relationship. There was no holding back with Jack. It had to be all or nothing. Jack was not a halfway person and neither was she. A little voice, which she recognized as the voice of temptation, said if they made love once, only once, then they'd have all summer to get over it.

"No, no, no," she muttered. What was she thinking?

"What?" he said.

"Nothing. I have to get back."

"You're the boss."

"No, I'm not. Not on this dig. I guess it's one reason I feel so relaxed." She wriggled her toes. "If this were my dig I'd be up there in my tent poring over the maps and the documents, making a schedule, assigning jobs, worrying about tomorrow. Instead…"

"Instead you're skinny-dipping with me, letting your worries float away. About time you took a break, don't you think? You've been working too hard these past few years."

Olivia stole a look in his direction. In the bright moonlight he appeared to be just making conversation and staring up at the stars. Still his "working too hard" comment stung. It was just what the fertility doctor had told them. Which had prompted her to take a leave of absence that did no good at all. She hoped Jack wasn't going to bring it up again. Best to set him straight.

"I didn't come to take a break, I came…"

"I know, you came because you want to find the lost tomb. Because you love the Hellenistic period and because you love finding lost treasures and because you can't resist a challenge."

He understood that much. They floated in silence for a long time, linked by the sea and by the past.

She hated to go back, but she had to. She had to get back to her tent and leave him outside on the ground. Not that he minded. Jack was so tough he could sleep on a slab of cement. She didn't want to break the bond they had tonight, so fragile, yet so strong it kept tugging at her.

The little voice inside her head kept saying, what was the harm of sleeping with Jack? They were married, after all. Half the people on this dig expected them to be having sex. Why shouldn't they?

Because, came the ready answer, of the consequences. At the end of the summer, the pain would be twice as bad as the last time, the parting that much more wrenching. Resolutely she turned and swam slowly back to shore.

Jack swam alongside. She'd always loved the water. Growing up she'd been a competitive swimmer in high school. But she hadn't ever swum nude at night until she met Jack, who'd been the one to unlock the sensual side to her she never knew she had.

She got to shore before he did and was already wearing her robe when he got out of the water.

She looked up at the moon, swaying a little, anything to avoid seeing his beautiful naked body.

"Anything wrong?" he asked, wrapping his robe around him.

"I think I got moonstruck out there," she said, her knees shaking. "Almost lost my bearings." She reached out for him to steady herself, and in an instant he'd pulled her into his arms and kissed her.

She wrapped her arms around his neck and kissed him back. He threaded one hand through her hair, cupping the back of her head, holding her steady so he could deepen the kiss. She could say it happened because she wasn't prepared, but that would be a lie. It happened because she wanted it to happen. She wanted to wrap her arms around his neck. She wanted him to devour her with his mouth. She wanted to feel his hard naked body against hers. But when she tried to untie the sash of her robe, her fingers wouldn't work. She felt feverish though her skin was cool.

She was losing touch with reality. She didn't know where she was or what day it was. Her pulse hammered in her veins. All she could think about was Jack, her husband, her love, her life. He tasted like saltwater and she couldn't get enough.

"Hey," a voice shouted from above. A bright beam swung across the sand and came to rest on them.

"Someone down there?"

"It's Stavros, the watchman," Jack muttered. "Just when we didn't need to be watched." He yelled up that they were okay. "Everything's fine, Stav," he shouted. His voice sounded raspy in the still night.

Everything was not fine. Jack stood staring blankly

at Olivia, his breath coming fast and furious. He couldn't believe what had happened, or what had almost happened. He'd been caught in a frenzy of passion. It had always been that way with them.

"Olivia," he said.

But she was putting her sandals on and in just seconds she was running across the sand to the path. Now it was his turn to stumble, racing up the path trying to catch her, breathing hard, to tell her he was sorry. Even though he wasn't. He banged his knee against a rock. He swore.

By the time he got to the grassy area under the trees, the watchman was still there but Olivia was gone.

"Sorry, Mr. Jack," the stocky watchman with the big mustache said, "I didn't know who it was."

"It's okay," Jack said, thumped him on the shoulder and went to find Olivia.

He stood outside her tent for a long moment. "Olivia, are you all right?"

"Good night, Jack."

The next morning Olivia got up early, full of resolve, and hurried to the food area. Thankfully she didn't see Jack or his sleeping bag. If she had she would have stepped over him and pretended he didn't exist. As if she could. As if it would do any good. He existed and she had to deal with it. She could and she would.

She knew better than to go off and swim with Jack. She knew what it could and would lead to. Someone had seen them. Sure, he was just the watchman and probably wouldn't tell anyone, but maybe the word would get out.

It was early, but already the air was hot and still. The crew hired to do the heavy digging started early and their shouts rang out before the students or the staff arrived. She cast a swift glance at the sea glittering in the sun below. The memory of last night's swim and what followed made her break out in a cold sweat despite the hot sun beating down on her.

The smell of the thick, sweet Greek coffee filled the air. She heard the students arrive on their noisy mopeds, and the chef began making American-style breakfasts of eggs, bacon and toast for them.

Olivia greeted the students and professors under the food tent, hoping she looked more rested than she was. A quick glance told her Jack wasn't around. She could only hope he'd eaten early and was already in the trenches digging or tapping with his pick at the rocky outside of the tomb. If he had any sense he'd realize they could not cavort around this work site like they had last night and he'd avoid her. She couldn't avoid him forever on her own, but every Jack-free minute of the day had to be a bonus and would help her regain her equanimity.

When she saw Dr. Robbins, she made a quick decision and asked him to transfer her to another team.

"Instead of digging, I'd really like to be reassigned to do the cleaning of the objects up here under the tent," she said. "I've had a good deal of experience setting up the system with the brushes, acid, etcetera and cataloging of course."

"Is it claustrophobia?" Robbins asked with a concerned look on his kindly face.

"Oh, no," she said. "Well, maybe just a touch." He was right. She was a little claustrophobic especially in some of the very small enclosed spaces. But since that was a big part of excavating, she'd never let it hold her back before. "I just think I can be more useful up here."

"Of course. I appreciate that. Your expertise is most welcome, my dear Mrs. Oakley. We're delighted to have you along this summer."

Olivia felt a rush of relief. This way she could put some space between her and Jack. "Please call me Olivia," she said. If one more person called her Mrs. Oakley, she'd scream.

She went to the makeshift buffet table where she reached for some fresh crusty bread the chef had taken out of his wood-fired oven, along with some tangy feta cheese and a handful of olives then sat on a bench next to Fred, Jack's student. There was something so satisfying about a Greek breakfast. And a Greek lunch or a Greek dinner. There was something about Greece that made her ravenously hungry.

Fred and the other students talked about dancing and drinking in the clubs the night before.

"You should have come," Fred said to Olivia. "Those Greeks are amazing. Dancing the *syrtaki* and drinking ouzo like there's no tomorrow."

"Unfortunately there is a tomorrow and I guess I'm too old for that kind of thing," she said. It made her feel ancient to think about how she'd be retiring early every night all summer while they were out having a good time.

"No, you're not. Some of the Greeks are as old as you," he insisted.

"Who's as old as Olivia?" Jack said, taking a seat on the other side of Fred. Of course he looked as though he'd just spent a week in a health spa, his hair damp and smelling vaguely like Greek lemon-scented soap. Or did she just remember that's what he smelled like?

"No one," she said. "Except for the ancient Greeks. Fred was telling us about the fun they had last night in town."

"Really? We'll have to hit the clubs one night, too," he said with a glance at Olivia.

"Not me," she said, shooting daggers at him. What did she have to do to get him and the whole group to realize they were not a couple? "I brought a night-light so I can get my work done at night." How dare he insinuate they were still together in front of everyone.

"Everyone sleep well?" he asked with an expansive gesture.

While everyone at the table assured him they had, Olivia almost choked on her bread. Did he have to be so disgustingly cheerful in the morning? Or was it an act to convince her last night meant nothing to him? Her changing teams ought to convince him she felt the same.

She ate the last olive on her plate, then quickly got up to go talk to her new team and set up the tables for the recovery of the objects. She had to hope there would be objects to clean or even fragments to piece together. Even more she hoped Jack would not challenge her about her leaving his team.

She got both of her wishes. She didn't hear a word from Jack. Maybe he hadn't noticed she was missing or maybe he was glad she'd left his group. Whatever it was, she kept looking over her shoulder, but she didn't see him at all.

The other important thing was that the team that was digging along the south end of the site came up with pottery fragments just before noon. The students, dirty and dripping with sweat, were very excited, and though Olivia wasn't sure the pieces were important or even Hellenistic, she was glad to have something to do in analyzing them.

She'd entered the information into her computer, then got up to stretch. Everywhere there was activity. Faculty and students were digging or hauling dirt, surveying or marking off areas. Hired local men were digging a huge hole where the tomb should be. Should be but never was. Olivia remembered only too well the disappointment of the last summer they were there.

She went to splash cold water on her face from a hose hooked up to a well, and filled a cup with fresh cold water to drink.

"Any luck with that pottery?"

It was Jack, his new clothes she'd just bought him caked with dirt, a smile on his grimy face. If he'd missed her, he wasn't saying. Maybe she was wrong. Maybe they could have worked together. Maybe last night meant nothing to him, either. She might have acted too soon, and now it was too late to change her mind.

"I'm not sure. I think they're recent. Too soon to say,

really. Hate to tell the students they're too new to be important. They were so excited. How are you doing?" she asked. What if he'd found something important and she wasn't there?

"These workers they hired are great. They actually started last week before we got here, and they've already gone farther into the tunnel than we did last time. It's looking good. Very good."

She heard the controlled excitement in his voice. He wouldn't say anything unless he was sure, but she could tell when he was on to something. She felt a shiver of excitement go up her spine.

"Sorry to hear about your claustrophobia," he said.

"Oh, that. I thought it was under control, but…"

"But it came back last night, didn't it?" he asked, his eyes narrowed, the lines in his forehead deepening. "That's not all that came back. Admit it, Olivia, you and I are not finished."

CHAPTER SEVEN

OLIVIA worked all day under the tent. And the next day after that. And the next day. At night she retired to her tent, avoiding Jack whenever and wherever she could. Which wasn't that hard. She knew where he was. He was digging. When he was getting close to something, he was like a man possessed.

Of course she was curious. But she didn't want to ask him, especially after his last comment, *You and I are not finished.* A comment that made her seethe with anger. Since then she'd thought of a dozen retorts, but hadn't had a chance to verbalize even one.

She was convinced Jack would tell her if he'd found anything significant. If he hadn't, there was nothing more to say, except for something personal, so she kept her distance, and he was making it easy for her to do just that.

At night she saw the lights on around the site and she knew they'd strung them down into the tunnel, too. She pictured Jack down there, tapping away with his pick. She was glad she wasn't down there with him, working with him at close quarters.

She needed a break from him. When the generator ran late, keeping the power going and the lights on, she would lie in her sleeping bag listening to the rumble of the motor, thinking about him, picturing him alone in the tunnel, scraping away at the stone, looking for that elusive burial chamber.

Sometimes she felt she should be there with him, sharing the work and the possibility of finding something big. Mostly she was glad she wasn't. Sometimes she didn't know what she wanted.

As for her work, she'd collected a few pieces of glass, many shards of pottery, and one of the students brought her a coin, but it was clearly Roman. Not that she wasn't interested, but it wasn't as significant or rare as an earlier coin would have been.

Lunch on the fifth day was a delicious buffet where the crew ate whenever they could take a break. She sat next to Marilyn and three students eating pasta, grilled fresh fish just caught off the reef below them and stuffed tomatoes.

"I'm going to gain a kilo this summer," Marilyn complained good-naturedly as she reached for a piece of pita bread. "This food is too good."

The chef came by in his white toque and apron and accepted their compliments. He said he'd made a special lunch because he was off that night. He had promised to work a special dinner at the Corinth Café in town, where he used to be until Dr. Robbins offered him more money to cook for them this summer.

Olivia hoped Jack wouldn't get too engrossed in digging and forget to eat lunch again. He could do that.

She never saw him eat dinner last night. She used to have to remind him at mealtime. No more. She wasn't responsible for him. He'd done fine without her these past few years. Still, she couldn't help wondering exactly where he was, how he was, what he'd found.

"So tonight I am cooking for a big party at the café in honor of St. Andrew, the patron saint of Hermapolis," the chef said. "The director suggests you go to town to enjoy the festival. Eat, drink and dance in the streets."

"Sounds like fun," Marilyn said, and the students echoed her enthusiasm.

"First I've heard of it," Olivia murmured. She had no intention of going to a festival, to eat, drink and dance in the streets. Especially if Jack was going. She'd been to other festivals with him after they were married and she knew how they ended up.

The music, the rhythm, the dancing, the party atmosphere. They'd get so carried away they barely made it back to their hotel room to make mad, passionate love. Her face felt hot and she had trouble catching a breath just thinking about it. Oh, yes, it had happened before and she couldn't let it happen again. Not this summer.

So when the sun set turning the hills to gold and the sea to silver, she stood watching the group go, the professors in the van, the students on their mopeds. And Jack? Nowhere to be seen.

Fred came up to her, wheeling his moped.

"Come on, Mrs. Oakley. I mean Olivia," he said. "Hop on, I'll give you a ride to town."

"I don't think so." She looked around. She was the

only one left. Why should she stay there like some old crone when she was not that much older than these grad students? Especially if Jack wasn't going. She'd be safe and she wouldn't even remember how she'd once upon a time ended up in his bed. She shouldn't even give him a thought. It was clear he didn't give one to her. What was the problem? Yes, she'd go.

Tonight she'd walk around town, sit down in a taverna and watch the crowds, then catch a ride back in a van later.

"Okay," she said, "if you can wait just a minute."

In her tent, she dumped her shorts on the ground, took off her bra and changed into a white dress with a form-fitting bodice and spaghetti straps and a pair of sandals. Then she knotted a sweater around her shoulders. Her aunt Alyce would be proud of her. "About time you had some fun," she'd say. "Let loose and do something besides work for a change."

Fred grinned when he saw her. He was a cute guy. No doubt he'd land one of the girls on the crew this summer. Maybe tonight. Olivia could vouch for the romantic atmosphere.

Jack came staggering out of the tunnel that led to the tomb just in time to see Olivia ride off on the back of Fred's moped, her skirt trailing in the wind. He'd been crawling around for hours, scraping away at the stone walls. What wouldn't he give for a hot soak for his tired muscles.

He stood there, hot and tired and hungry and covered with dirt. Damn it, he was the only one on this dig with any work ethic. Olivia of all people, leaving on the back of some guy's bike without even telling him she was going.

He jumped into the shower, letting the cold water wash away the dirt but not his anger. He ran into Stavros on his way to his sleeping bag where he'd have to change clothes in the open because Olivia had taken over the tent.

"Where has everyone gone?" he asked.

"To the festival, boss," the watchman said. "You go, too?"

"I don't know. Yeah, sure." What festival? He'd been out of touch since he'd starting digging in earnest. It was easier to bury himself in his work than trying to talk to Olivia. After she'd switched to a different team without even telling him, it was clear she didn't want to socialize or work with him.

Everyone else thought the tomb was at the far end of the excavation. He didn't. Which left him to dig alone without interference. He'd lose track of time. Come up and lunch would be over. He'd find something to eat and go back down. No wonder he hadn't heard about the festival. His fault. He'd done nothing but work since that night on the beach.

He looked around. It was just him and Stavros. If he wanted anything to eat he'd better go to town, too, festival or not.

He changed into clean khakis and a white shirt and drove to town in the Jeep. He parked just off the main square, which was roped off. All the tavernas, coffee shops, bars and restaurants had extended seating out into the square. There was live music coming from everywhere, people walking, sitting, standing, eating and dancing.

He circled the square once before he saw her. She was sitting with Fred at a table, looking carefree and animated. What about all the work she was supposed to be doing at night? What about her being "too old" for this kind of fun? He clamped his jaw shut tight in frustration. She was his wife, dammit. He shouldn't be out looking for her. She shouldn't be out with some student. This was not the way it was supposed to be.

When she saw him threading his way between the tables her eyebrows shot up. Fred turned and waved to him.

"Dr. Oakley," he said. "I didn't know you were coming."

"Obviously," Jack said with a sharp glance at Olivia.

Fred stood, looking nervous, as if he'd been caught with the boss's wife. "Can I get you something to drink, like a glass of retsina?"

"Sure," Jack said, grabbing a chair and sitting down across from Olivia.

He glared at her. "You could have told me you were coming here."

"I didn't know where you were," she said.

"Digging, that's where I was. Funny, I thought you would be there, too. We were on the same team, remember?"

"I thought it would be better if I stayed up above, checking out the artifacts as they find them."

"Better or easier? If you're afraid of going underground say so. You never used to let your claustrophobia get to you."

"It doesn't get to me."

"Then it must be me you don't want to work with."

"Not everything is about you, Jack." She picked up her wineglass and took a sip. He was glad to see her hand wasn't all that steady. So he did have some effect on her, but he was afraid it wasn't a positive effect.

A waiter went by with a tray of savory pizza covered with olives and feta cheese. He had the waiter cut slices for himself and Olivia and Fred. "If he comes back," Jack muttered, looking around the café. For a few minutes they devoured the crisp pizza with the rich sauce without talking, as if they hadn't eaten all day. Jack hadn't had much since breakfast, which was before anyone else was up, and he was ravenous.

The Greeks had taken Italian pizza and made it their own savory dish, with the black olives and the sharp white cheese crumbled on top of the crisp yeasty dough. Jack reached for her wine, drained the glass, sat back in his chair and looked at her. She was wearing a dress he'd never seen. Her hair hung smooth and straight to her bare shoulders. She looked like a carefree tourist, not an archaeologist. A very beautiful tourist who was having a wonderful vacation. Without him.

"Having a good summer?" he asked, his voice dripping with sarcasm.

"Very good," she said coolly, her chin in the air. "Nice people, interesting site, what more could a person want?"

"I don't know. I thought you wanted to find the tomb."

"Of course I do. I'm doing my part even though I'm not down there with a pick in my hand. I assume you'll tell me and everyone else if you find something where you're digging. Where *are* you digging?"

"At the south end." He signaled to the waiter and ordered two more glasses of wine. "Your date seems to have deserted you," he said.

"Don't be ridiculous. He's not my date. He gave me a ride here and he bought me a glass of wine. Just a courtesy to one of his elders."

"Elders? You look like a college girl," he said, his gaze taking in her wide-set dark eyes, her smooth shoulders and the swell of her breasts under her dress.

"You didn't know me as a college girl. I wore baggy sweatpants, thick glasses and my hair back like this." She pulled her hair away from her face into a knot at the back of her neck.

He frowned, trying to imagine her as anything but gorgeous, glasses or not, then he took a drink of the wine the waiter brought.

"If you'd known me, you wouldn't have given me the time of day."

"I like to think I can see beyond the surface."

"And you, Mr. Fraternity Hotshot, would have appreciated my intellect and my disregard for style along with my love of the past?"

He slouched uncomfortably in the wrought-iron chair. "Of course. Along with your beautiful hair. It's the color of honey, Greek honey."

She looked down at her plate. He could see the blush rise in her face.

"You've always had a problem with compliments."

"I have not." She looked up at him. "If I have, it's because they're often shameless flattery and attempts to get something. Also because looks weren't valued in my family, only brains."

"Except for your aunt Alyce of course."

"She's different. Always has been. She spends a fortune on her looks. There's her day spa and her hairdresser…"

"Come on, you two, we're dancing in the square." Fred had returned to the table and was standing in front of them and holding out his hands.

Jack jumped to his feet, ignored the twinge in his back, grabbed Olivia's hand and pulled her out to the terrace. Amplified bouzouki music filled the air. The cafés and tavernas were emptying as the patrons and the waiters all rushed out en masse to join hands and dance the *syrtaki*.

Olivia gripped Jack's hand tightly. The music filled the square and seeped right into her soul. She knew what the music meant to the Greeks; it was all about love and loss, and hope, too.

It wasn't easy keeping her distance from Jack this week. Every day at lunch she'd looked for him, and every night at dinner. He never came. She worried about him. But she never asked about him. She didn't want anyone to think she cared. If she had expressed any of her concern for his welfare, they would have just shrugged and said, "That's Jack."

It didn't used to be him. He used to make time to eat and drink and talk. And make love to her. She missed that. She'd never admit it to him, but she missed it all, especially making love. Having him so close yet so far caused an ache deep inside her. Even worse, it caused her to regret coming on this dig. She thought she could handle it, but maybe she'd overestimated her inner strength.

Swaying with the music, she slid a glance in Jack's direction. The intense look in his eyes when his gaze met hers sent shock waves right through her. She knew that look. He didn't try to hide the lust. She knew what it did to her. She tried to pull away, but he tightened his grip on her hand.

She couldn't blame the wine for their getting caught up in the frenzy. She hadn't had that much. Neither had he. She couldn't blame Jack for insisting she dance. She couldn't blame Fred for suggesting it, either. That left only herself and her weak will to blame for letting desire rush through her veins and take over. It was like a fire burning out of control. Like a torch, an inferno. She wanted him. If he asked her to go with him now, anywhere, she would have been helpless to say no.

When the music finally stopped she was still under its spell, and all rational thought was long gone. It was then they ran into Dr. Robbins and his wife.

"Saw you two dancing," he said. "How's your back?" he asked Jack.

Olivia shot an anxious look at Jack, but he brushed off the question.

Her hand still clasped tightly in Jack's, Olivia wanted to follow up and ask what was wrong with his back, but she didn't. Next Robbins asked them to drive him and his wife back to the hotel. Which was how she was sitting next to Jack in the front seat of the Jeep with the Robbinses in the back. Somehow the rest of them were all chatting normally about the dig and the festival while her heart was hammering. All she could think about was Jack sitting next to her, one hand on the steering wheel, the other on her bare knee. Reminding her of what those hands could do. How they could make her feel.

They pulled up in front of the hotel and got out of the Jeep. The Robbinses thanked them and went to their cottage, and she and Jack walked through the hotel and onto the patio overlooking the sea. The hunger in his eyes made her break out in goose bumps all over her bare arms. He put his hands on her shoulders and kissed her, hard and hot. She kissed him back. Her hands shook; her legs were like Jell-O. He put one hand on his hip and grimaced.

"What's wrong with your back?" she asked, gasping for breath.

"Nothing."

"Did you pull a muscle?"

"Yeah, maybe. Just a spasm. It'll pass."

"You need to stop working so hard. And sleeping on the ground." She felt a pang of guilt.

"What I need is a hot bath and a back rub."

There was a long silence full of unspoken thoughts shimmering in the night air. The images of other nights, her hands on his back, his hands on her came rushing back like a tidal wave. They both knew where this was leading. It was a steam roller, a train out of control. Just let anyone try to stop it.

She knew they shouldn't do this. She knew she couldn't resist temptation, but for the life of her she couldn't think why she shouldn't. They were married. They were together again, at least for the summer, they didn't have to consider anyone but themselves and they were tough. If they got hurt when it was over, if they were let down at the end of the summer, well, there were worse things. The worst thing she could think of right now was not spending the night with Jack. Her heart was ricocheting in her chest, her face was flaming. She had to have Jack and she had to have him now. ˋ

"Why don't you…" Her voice trailed off.

In minutes Jack was back with the key to room 103, their room. She didn't know anyone with a back spasm could move so fast.

The next morning Jack sat on the deck staring off at the bright-blue sea, dazed and happier than he'd been in months, no years. It was a night he would never forget. It was the past and the present and promises of the future all rolled into one.

He was trying not to overanalyze what had happened. Just letting it sink in slowly. He and Olivia were back together. After a night like that, how could they not be?

He hadn't realized how much he'd missed her, how incomplete he'd been without her until now. But after last night…the world was a different place. Anything was possible. They would get back together. They had to. He would make any sacrifice to make it happen.

When she came out on the deck in her dress from last

night, barefoot with her hair damp from the shower, he felt a wave of pride and possession overwhelm him. His wife, his love, his life. Olivia. Forever.

"After a night in this chair and a night in that bed, I can tell you, the bed's better," he said with a grin.

"We have to talk," she said. Her brow was lined, her voice was strained.

His grin faded. He didn't much like the sound of that.

"What about?"

"Us. Last night was…"

"Incredible."

"Something we have to put behind us."

"Why?"

"Why? I don't have to tell you why. The same reason we split up. Because we don't have a future together or a present. All we have is a past. We have our own lives now. We have our own work. We're getting divorced."

He stood. A hot, shooting pain hit him in the small of his back. Real or psychological? He winced. "Divorced? After last night? How can you say that? It doesn't have to be that way."

"Yes, it does."

"No, it doesn't. I'll come back to Santa Clarita, I'll take any job they'll give me, lecturer, assistant professor, whatever."

"After you've been department chairman? You'd be miserable, taking orders from someone else."

"Then you come to Cal. I'll give you a job, any job you want." He had to talk fast or she'd get carried away with this ridiculous idea they didn't belong together.

"I have the job I want."

He stared at her in disbelief. "Did last night mean anything to you?"

"Of course. It was…fine, okay, incredible, like you said. But it was one night. And it shouldn't have happened. I didn't mean for it to happen. It's my fault, I got carried away. There won't be any more like that."

"You can say that again," he muttered darkly.

"Then there's the fact that I can't have children," she said stiffly.

"That's not a problem," he said. "We don't need children. You don't want to give up your career to stay home with kids and neither do I. Think of the ferry accident, think of all the mishaps we've been through. Kids would just get in the way. We have too much to do, and we have each other."

She looked at him as if he'd lost his mind, when she was the one who was overreacting. What was wrong with her? After they'd finally gotten back together, she decided they hadn't? He marshaled his arguments. She couldn't keep them apart. She had to come around and agree to a future together.

She shook her head. "No," she said. "We don't."

There was a knock on the door and a waiter came in with a tray of strong hot coffee, a pitcher of hot milk and a platter of flaky pastries. He set it on the deck between them.

Jack looked at the food as if it was made of plastic. A moment ago he'd been starving. Now his stomach was in knots, his throat was raw and his back was killing him. But Olivia was carefully pouring the coffee as if she were at a tea party. Steady as a rock. What had happened to the warm passionate woman he'd made love to last night?

"You've got to eat something, Jack," she said. "You look terrible."

"Thanks," he said dryly. "For nothing."

CHAPTER EIGHT

OLIVIA didn't think it would be easy to avoid Jack during the weeks that followed, but it was. He was on his own schedule. He worked early and late. He avoided the meals the group ate together, and she surmised he ate leftovers whenever he came up from digging in the tunnel. Sometimes she'd see him on the periphery of her vision but then he was gone before she could speak to him. She wanted to talk to him, to make sure he understood her position. Because when they'd left the hotel that morning he'd clammed up and refused to speak to her. Why couldn't he understand how hard it was for her to make the decision she had, but that it was for the best?

She didn't have to see him to know he was around. She knew: a sudden wave of heat flooded her cheeks; her skin tingled. So much for her peace of mind. She had to work on that. Try harder to forget that magic night at the hotel and all the other nights she'd spent with him. Because it was over. Really over at last. This way it would be easier to say goodbye at the end of the summer. For both of them. She was finally clear on the future. Nothing could make her change her mind.

"How're you doing?" he asked casually one day, dropping by the tent where she was sorting and classifying objects.

She almost jumped out of her seat. This time he'd surprised her. "Fine." Her voice sounded high and tinny in her ears.

"You look tired," he said, giving her a close look. She wished he wouldn't do that. He could always see beyond the surface and she had no defenses against him.

"I'm not." But she was. Who wouldn't be tired lying awake at night thinking of him, worrying about him sleeping on the hard ground with his sore back. "How's your back?" she asked.

He shrugged.

"What are you doing down there?"

"Digging for a lost tomb."

"I know that. But everyone else thinks it's at the other end of the site."

"What everyone else thinks doesn't concern me."

That was Jack to a T. Stubborn, dedicated, obsessed. When he had an idea, he stuck to it. Which was why she was surprised he'd accepted her decision so easily. He'd never said another word about it. In fact he'd barely said another word to her about anything at all.

She'd expected an argument. She'd lain awake at night composing her thoughts. For nothing. He must have finally realized she was right. She was relieved, or she ought to be.

"Look at this piece," she said. She held up a broken pendant, and it slipped out of her fingers. So much for acting normal, as if he was just another colleague. "What do you think?"

He ran his finger over the surface. "Could be Bronze Age. From the old site under the other sites." He turned to go, but she didn't want him to leave. She might not see him again for a week or more. She'd missed him. She didn't want to but she had. Missed their discussions and missed their arguments.

"Wait, I've hardly seen you," she said.

"Isn't that what you wanted?"

"Of course, but I still want to be friends."

He laughed harshly. "I don't think so."

"Why not?"

"You're asking me?"

"I never said I didn't want to…to…keep in touch. I'm just trying to make things easier for both of us."

"Make things easier for yourself, if you want, but leave me out of it."

"If you had told me you were coming this summer…"

"You wouldn't have come, right?"

"I don't know, but at least I would have been prepared."

He leaned down until he was only an inch from her face. His eyes were blazing, the thin scar under his chin an instant reminder of an accident in a cave in Rhodes.

"How do you do that, Olivia? How do you prepare? By building a stone wall around yourself the way you've done? If you know how, you should write a book for the rest of the world. Because I sure as hell don't get it. I don't understand you. I thought I did, but I don't."

He turned and stalked off. Hot tears stung her eyes. He hated her. He thought she was cold and heartless. He didn't know how hard this was for her. How much she wanted him, despite everything. What was wrong with him? Couldn't he see she was doing this for his own good as well as hers? Obviously not. He'd just as good as told her to back off.

She rubbed her eyes with the back of her hand and left a trail of centuries-old dry dirt on her cheek.

"Mrs.? Something wrong?"

It was Elias, looking so concerned she gave him a watery smile.

"Come to the beach. I want to show you."

"What is it, Elias?"

He tugged at her hand. "Come."

She stood and put her arm around his shoulders. "Okay." She'd been working too hard. No wonder she felt like crying. Though surrounded by colleagues and students all day long, she'd never felt so lonely in the weeks since they'd made love at the hotel. She missed Jack and she missed him more than ever though he was only a few dozen yards away. She missed him so much there was a pain in her chest above her heart. The heart he thought she didn't have.

She and Elias jumped, slid and climbed down the path to the beach. Tied up to the new dock was a gleaming white cabin cruiser. So they'd finally repaired the dock and gotten a boat. The boat she and Jack were going to take to another island.

"Oh, very nice," Olivia said.

"No, not that. Look at me." Elias began skipping stones like a pro into the calm clear water.

"That's great," she said. "You've been practicing."

"And Mr. Jack, he show me."

"Yes, I remember."

"No, every day."

"Jack comes down here every day with you?"

"Nice man. Mr. Jack your husband, yes?"

"Yes, I mean no. Not really."

He looked puzzled. She didn't blame him; she was puzzled, too. His little mouth turned down. He threw another stone into the water. This time it just sank.

Olivia took off her shoes and socks and waded into the water. It felt so cool and soothing, she had to come down more often. As long as she didn't run into Jack. Jack who no longer wanted a child. Who thought they'd be in the way. To compensate he was spending his free time teaching someone else's son to skip stones. Again she felt helpless tears fill her eyes.

Elias was waving to someone on the cliff. "It's Mr. Jack," he said.

Olivia shaded her eyes with her hand, but there was no one there. The boy must be imagining him. Jack would be underground by now, digging and picking and shoveling like a man possessed.

Olivia climbed the path and cast a wistful look back at the boat from the top of the cliff. She'd never get a chance to go out on it now. Then she went back to work. If Jack could do it, so could she. If he found the lost tomb he'd forget about her and their argument. He'd realize she'd made the right decision.

He might find it all by himself. The way things were going, he'd probably keep it to himself and not share anything with her. He'd go back to Cal U, make a presentation, write a paper and get even more famous in the field than he already was. She didn't care. If he wanted to work that hard, let him. If he wanted to despise her, she couldn't stop him.

A few days later the mayor of the town invited the whole crew to a reception in their honor in the town square. With the memories of the last celebration still fresh in her mind, Olivia was determined not to go. She just wanted to be sure Jack went so they wouldn't be the only two left behind. That could be awkward.

"Sure you don't want to come?" Marilyn asked Olivia as dusk was falling over the farmland that surrounded the site.

"Positive. I'm really tired tonight. You have a great time. You look terrific," Olivia said, admiring the bright flared skirt and peasant blouse the older woman had bought in town the day they went shopping.

"What about Jack?"

Olivia looked around. She hadn't seen him at all. No surprise there. Maybe he didn't even know about the reception.

"I'm worried about him," Marilyn added. "He's

working too hard. And he's digging in the wrong place, by himself. Can't you talk to him?"

"Sure, I'll try," Olivia said. "If I see him." Yes, she could talk to Jack, but he wouldn't listen. She hoped she wouldn't see him. Not tonight. She was tired, and her defenses were weak. She'd take her journal, sit under a tree and write until it got too dark to see. Then she'd find something to eat in the food locker and retire to her tent. No dancing, no music, no making love.

Jack quickly climbed the ladder from the dirt floor of the excavation to the surface and looked around. He straightened his back and groaned. His muscles ached, his hands were caked with dirt and he was breathing hard. It wasn't late but it was getting dark and it was quiet. Everyone had gone to town. No one around except for Stavros, the watchman. He needed to see someone and he needed someone now. That someone was Olivia.

"Have you seen Olivia?" he asked the man.

"Everyone go to town, to big party. You not going, boss?" he asked.

"No."

"Cook save you some food."

"Good. Thanks."

"I can turn off generator now?"

"No," Jack said sharply. "Not yet. I need the lights down there. You want to leave? Go ahead. I can turn it off myself."

Stavros frowned.

"Go," Jack said. "It's okay." The man had a family and was already working late just for him. Reluctantly Stavros walked away toward his ancient pickup truck and stuck one hand out the side window to wave.

Jack went to Olivia's tent. Just in case. If she wasn't there he'd go to town to find her. He stood outside her tent. No way to knock on a tent flap. "Olivia?"

She stuck her head outside the flap and looked at him. Thank God she was there. She didn't look happy to see him; he was getting used to that. She'd be happier when she heard what he'd found.

"I have something to show you. It's…amazing."

"Can it wait till tomorrow? Then you can show everybody."

"I don't want to show everybody. Not until I'm sure. Why, are you busy?" He couldn't help the sarcasm in his voice. He said it was amazing. And she wanted to wait until tomorrow. What was wrong with her? Okay, she'd been avoiding him since that night at the hotel. He'd respected that. But this was different. This was business. "It's seven o'clock. What are you doing?"

"Does it matter?"

She was just sitting in her tent and she was too busy? "You have to come now."

"All right. But I can't stay long." She grabbed her flashlight and stepped out of the tent. "This better be good."

"It's good," he said flatly.

They walked across the field without speaking. Jack's head was spinning with the possibilities of the find. He couldn't believe his eyes. He had to get Olivia's opinion before he started celebrating. She followed him down the ladder to the first level of the site, then Jack pulled back the plywood panel painted red with the Keep Out warning sign in Greek.

He took her hand and led the way down a narrow low tunnel.

"This is it, this is where you've been digging by yourself?" she asked.

"Not myself. I've had help from the crew. Not everyone is working on the other end of the tunnel, in fact, a few more days and the other team and I will meet. That's why…"

"That's why you have to get there first, isn't it?"

"You think I'm competitive."

"I know you are. So am I. So is everyone here. But you're more so. You want to be the first one to find the lost tomb. That's why you give up vacations and you don't teach summer session where you could make more money. Is that it, have you found the tomb?" she asked. Her voice echoed eerily in the tunnel. They were in another world, his world now, where the surface noises were gone, and the air was cool and dry.

"Watch your head," he said, ignoring her question, "so you don't bump any of the ceiling beams."

"Guess I didn't need my flashlight," Olivia said, noting the wire along one side of the tunnel with a bare lightbulb every twenty feet.

"As long as the generator is running, the lights work."

Olivia felt a quiver of fear. The thin wire with its dim

bulbs was the only remaining link to the surface. She'd fought claustrophobia all her life. Just when she thought she'd beat it, it came rushing back. If anyone could help her forget it, it was Jack. She tightened her grip on his hand.

She stumbled on a large powdery mound of soil. Jack looked up at the ceiling, only an inch from his head. "This dirt has been sifting down through the rafters. I told the crew to cart it out." He kicked away some of the loose soil under their feet. "We're almost there."

Olivia shivered. The tunnel was only a few feet wide there. "This is it?" she asked.

"Not yet. Keep going, keep going. We're going to need more support work down here, braces on the walls and ceilings, before we can do any serious recovery, but I wanted to show you now what I found. I think you'll be impressed." A few minutes later, a few steps further walking in the loose dirt, Jack took her flashlight out of her hand and beamed it at a partially exposed slab of marble.

She gasped. It was a beautiful clear carving with a warm-honey patina. "Ohhhh," she said softly.

"It's funerary stele, isn't it?" he asked.

"Yes, yes, I think so," she said, stepping toward it, unable to keep the excitement out of her voice, even though she didn't know, wasn't sure...

"Damn, more dust and rock have come down just in the last hour." Jack brushed some dust from the marble to expose the partial figure of a woman and an inscription. "Can you read it?"

Olivia ran her fingers over the Greek letters as Jack

pushed the soil away. Eagerly she made out a word, then another. "In the year 293, month of…"

She shook her head. The rest of the letters were covered with dirt. It was maddening. She raised her arm to brush away the dirt and dislodged a small rock above them. It rolled down and hit a post which suddenly shifted. Small rocks and dust tumbled down on their heads. Olivia gagged as the dust filled her nose and mouth.

"Get down." Jack pushed Olivia to one side to escape the falling rocks, then slammed his head into a low overhead beam and dropped the flashlight. He swore.

"You okay?" he asked her, staggering to his knees on the dirt where she was crouched, her arms around her knees.

"Uh-huh. How bad is it?" she asked, her voice small and shaky.

A shower of rocks cascaded down on both of them, bouncing off their heads, arms and shoulders. It was the answer to her question neither wanted to hear. An answer they'd heard before. It was bad. Very bad.

"We'll get out of this," he said. "We always do. Remember the caves in Basilicotta? No one thought we'd make it, but we swam out at high tide. We can do it again."

She glanced at him. Did he really believe that or was he just trying to reassure her? She wanted to believe him, but…

"Kind of hard to swim in the dirt," she said, fighting off tears. Whatever she did, she couldn't let Jack know how scared she was. It was bad enough struggling against claustrophobia, imagining the dirt walls caving in on them. Now it had happened. It was no longer a phobia. Her worst fears had become reality. The walls were caving in on her.

"We have to get out now." She put one hand on his shoulder and struggled to stand.

With a crash the overhead beam that was holding the lightbulb above them fell a few inches away from her head. The tunnel was plunged into darkness. It was the end. They'd never get out of there alive. Olivia clamped her mouth shut to keep from screaming.

When she finally opened her mouth she choked and coughed and spit the dust out. In the distance she could hear more rocks falling.

"You all right?" Jack asked, his voice only inches away.

She wiped the dust from her face and swallowed hard. "I think so. What happened?"

"Might have an idea if I could see," Jack said. "I can't find the flashlight." Silently cursing his carelessness, he clawed in the rubble around them. Finally a wisp of light appeared in the dirt, and he grabbed the flashlight. First he shone it on Olivia, who was covered with dirt, her pale face staring at him, her eyes wide with fear. He reached out to touch her cheek.

"We'll get out of this," he said.

She managed a weak smile. "You always were an optimist."

"Only way to go," he said. Then he directed the beam of light around the passageway and saw the extent of the problem. Oh God, it was worse than he thought. Optimist yes. But he was also a realist.

"Damn," he said, his jaw locked tight. "These last two rafters have come down. Look at that pile of rock. Who knows if the others are still standing."

"So," she said. "What are our options?"

Good for Olivia. Thinking clearly despite her fears. Sounding rational and being practical in the midst of chaos. If only there were any options.

"There's not enough room at this end for us to dig," he said as matter-of-factly as he could. "We're walled in. They'd have to do most of the digging from the other end."

"They? Who's they? Everyone's gone to town. No one's here. No one will be back until morning. We can't…"

"Don't say can't," he said gruffly. "If only I hadn't sent Stavros home. He'd notice if the line was shorted, because it would blow the breaker on the generator. He'd figure I was down here. Then when I didn't come up, he'd come down and call the crew, start digging. But…"

"But you did and he's gone?"

"I didn't want him to be late for dinner." He coughed. "His wife hates when that happens."

"We can't hold out until tomorrow, Jack. There's not much air and what there is is awful."

He shone the light in her face. She looked amazingly calm. Anyone else would be in hysterics, blaming him and demanding he do something. Olivia was not any other woman. There was no use pretending, no use lying to her. She was too smart.

"You may be right," he said. The flashlight dimmed and went out. The tunnel was dark again.

CHAPTER NINE

"I WANT to tell you how sorry I am," Jack said after long moments of silence while they both realized how slim the chances were of getting out of there. "For what I said before I left. I accused you of being a quitter."

"I was. I quit trying to get pregnant."

Jack shook his head even though he knew she couldn't see him. "No, you gave it your all."

"I never told you, but that's why I didn't want to have sex anymore. It had to be done at certain times and for one reason only. It got to be like a job. I hated it, but I couldn't let you know."

"Yes, you could. You should have told me."

"I was afraid of hurting your feelings. We'd been so close. I knew you so well. I could tell you wanted out. Don't deny it."

"I thought a change of scene would be good for me, for us. But you wouldn't come with me. Don't say I didn't ask you. I shouldn't have to ask you. I expected you to pack up and come with me. Instead you decided to stay and you even seemed relieved I was leaving."

"I was. I couldn't stand to see you look at me as if I'd let you down."

"For God's sake, Olivia, you've never let me down."

"What about that farewell party?"

"I don't give a damn about the party. Sure, everyone asked where you were. I said you had the flu. That's not what bothered me."

"What did? Go ahead. We're never going to get out of here alive. I want to know what made you leave," she said.

"It bothered me that you wouldn't talk to me about what bothered you. Hell, you wouldn't talk to me about anything."

"Anything? I talked to you all the time," she protested.

"Not about the important things. The baby we didn't have. The vacations we didn't take. The time we didn't make for each other. The subjects we never talked about. The resentment you felt," he said, "when I got promoted and you didn't."

"I was proud of you," she said, "but…"

"Go on. But what?"

"But I guess I was jealous, too. I wanted to make full professor. I wanted the time off for research, too. You make it look so easy." There was such sadness in her voice, he wrapped his arm around her shoulders and pulled her close.

"You said I was arrogant and self-serving," he said.

"I shouldn't have."

"No, you were right. I was full of myself. You made it easy for me to succeed. You were my support team, my backup. I couldn't have done it without you. I never thanked you. I never told you that, did I?" he asked, suddenly overcome with regret.

"No," she said. "You got along fine without me at Cal though."

"I thought I did. Until now. Now I realize how empty my life there has been. Oh, sure, I have my students and the work is great, but at the end of the day, there's no one to share it with. There's no you." His voice dropped.

"Jack, I have to tell you something."

"I know, you filed for divorce."

"Why didn't you sign the papers?"

"I couldn't do it. I couldn't give up on us until I gave it another try."

"So that's what this dig is all about?"

"Not entirely. There is this tomb." He gave a hollow laugh. "But yes, I had to think up a dig that would intrigue you, that you couldn't pass up."

"That's not what I want to tell you," she said. "I put the house on the market before I left."

"Our house? You're selling our house?"

"It's *my* house. That's what you said before you left. That you wouldn't be back," she reminded him. "And it was all mine."

"I said a lot of things I didn't mean."

"Like my being too sensitive, too thin-skinned, too tense." She couldn't deny the words had hurt.

"I was hoping you'd forgotten all that," Jack said. "As soon as I said them, I wished I could take the words back. I've missed you, Olivia. I can't tell you how much."

"Jack, I can't lie to you. I was glad you left. I

couldn't stand the tension anymore. It wasn't your fault, but I knew how much you wanted that baby. Making love became a chore. Everything you said, I interpreted as criticism. I can't ever go back to our old life. That's why I'm selling the house. Your office, your closet, your bookshelves, they're all a reminder of the failure of our marriage."

"I'm not asking you to go back to our old life. I want a new life with you."

"Isn't it too late for that?" she asked softly. Even if they reconciled, they were not going to get out of this tunnel alive.

He didn't say anything. Olivia couldn't see him, but she felt his hip wedged next to hers, his hand on her shoulder.

What could he say? No more words of sunny optimism about a happy future for them. There was no point. She knew as well as Jack did the chances of their getting out of there were practically zero. If she had to die on a dig, she'd prefer to die with Jack. No matter how much he'd hurt her in the past. He was her soul mate. Now, it looked like she was going to get her wish.

"I just want to tell you again how sorry I am," he said roughly.

"For what? Bringing me down here? It was worth it. You did the right thing. That funerary is an amazing find, beautifully preserved. It means the tomb is here, and if I could have read the rest of the inscription we'd know who's buried here."

"So if we don't get out of here…"

Her lower lip trembled. If Jack didn't think they'd get

out of there, then there really was no hope. "You always said anything worth doing involves risks."

"I've gone too far this time."

"No, you're right. That's what I loved about you, your willingness to risk everything to get what you wanted."

"That's what this trip was all about," he said.

"You risked it all to get to the tomb."

"I risked it all to get you back. I had no right to bring you here under false pretenses. But I knew if I told you, you wouldn't come."

"Maybe not, but I'm glad I did. I love you, Jack." Now the tears were falling so fast she couldn't wipe them away. "If I have to die, I want to die with you."

"That's not going to happen," he said, slamming his fist into the dirt.

"But if it does…"

"I'm sorry I never took you on a honeymoon."

"There was no time."

"We could have made time."

"Where would we have gone?" she asked.

"I always wanted to go to Bali."

"The temples are right out there on the surface," she said pensively. "Sure that's enough challenge for you?"

"No digging. That's rather appealing at this point," he said dryly.

She sighed. If she ever got to the surface of the earth again, she'd never leave.

"The temples are old," she said. "Some have been in constant use since the stone age."

"Nice beaches."

"Friendly people."

"Is it a date?" he asked.

"It's too late. It was seven years ago." She rested her head on his shoulder. Neither stated the obvious. It *was* too late. Too late for them. Even if they lived, it was probably too late to make their marriage work.

Every breath she took felt as if it might be her last. She couldn't tell Jack. Couldn't let him know how terrified she was. She'd told him she loved him. Did he still love her?

"Seven years," he said. "Seems like yesterday." He traced the outline of her cheek with his fingers. "What about Machu Picchu?"

"I always wanted to go there," she said wistfully. "Imagine how Hiram Bingham felt climbing that mountain in Peru and discovering it in 1912."

"Like I felt when I fell in love with you," he said soberly. "That I'd found a new world."

"Maybe we should have tried again," she said.

"To have a baby?"

"No," she said. "I can't ever do that again. If that's what you want…"

"I don't want a baby, I want you. But I can't change, Olivia. I'll always be the arrogant, self-centered jerk you said I was."

"And I'll always be the quitter you said I was."

"And I'll always love you anyway."

He reached for her hand and squeezed it tight. "You're not wearing your ring."

The ring with "forever" inscribed on the inside of the band. "No. It was a reminder of how I'd failed."

"*We'd* failed."

"Maybe we gave up too easily," she said sadly. What she meant was *she'd* given up on their marriage too easily.

"My fault. I should never have left you."

"No, mine. I should have gone with you."

"The reason I came on this trip was to be with you again, work with you again. To convince you we belong together."

"Are you sure?" she asked anxiously. "Sure you don't want kids anymore, because…"

"I've never been surer of anything. They'd just be in the way. Besides, I don't want to share you with anyone."

"So if we get out of here…"

"Not if, when."

"Jack, be honest. I can take it. What are the chances?"

He didn't speak for a long moment. "Not good," he admitted, "but not impossible. If we can hold out until tomorrow."

Hold out until tomorrow? When the air was getting warmer and stuffier every minute? When the oxygen level was down to almost zero? He was just trying to make her feel better. She couldn't let him know it wasn't working. She had to play along. Act like there was hope. She was almost glad the flashlight had gone out. It was easier not to see the worried look on his face or the walls around them, the ceiling above them or the dirt below. Anything to keep the claustrophobia at bay.

"Whatever happens I'm glad I came back to Hermapolis," she said.

"Are you sure?" he asked, brushing a layer of dust from the top of her head.

"About the night at the hotel," she said.

"I take it you had second thoughts," he said. "You were angry with me."

"I was angry at myself for giving in. I was determined to keep my distance from you. I wanted nothing to do with you."

"I noticed," he said.

"I knew that at the end of the summer it would be the end of the line for us. You'd sign the papers and our divorce would go through. If we got together this summer, even for one night, I'd be hurt all over again. But it happened and I knew I'd made a terrible mistake."

"You still think so?"

"I don't know, Jack. I don't know. I can't help loving you, but I can help what I do about it."

"Do about it? You don't have to do anything. Let me do it, let me fix it, whatever it takes. Just tell me you're not sorry for that night."

She couldn't speak, for a long moment. All she could think about was how she'd felt that night, how the past and the present had come together when they made love. How she'd finally felt complete again in his arms.

"Who was it that said, you never regret the things you do, only the things you didn't do? That's how I feel," she said. She tucked her hand through his arm, feeling his strength, drawing courage from him, wishing she could give some back.

"What was that?" Jack said, leaning forward. "Did you hear something?"

"No, nothing." Now she was really scared. Jack was starting to hallucinate. Wanting so badly to think someone was coming to get them, he was actually hearing things.

"Shh, listen," Jack said. When it came, the voice was so weak it was barely audible. But it was real. His heart banged against his rib cage. Hope rose in his throat and threatened to choke him. It was Stavros.

His feeble voice filtered through the piles of rock blocking the tunnel. "Jack, are you down there?"

Olivia felt tears rush to her eyes.

"It's Stavros," Jack said to Olivia, grabbing her arm and kissing her on the cheek. "We're here," he shouted. "We're okay. No injuries. How far away are you?"

"Post Twelve," Stavros shouted. "Sixty meters. The tunnel is blocked here. Are you in the clear?"

He shouted an affirmative. "Thank God," he said to Olivia. "If he's sixty meters in, that means there's less than ten meters of blockage."

He didn't mention the possibility that the entire tunnel might be filled with rubble, but he'd thought about it. It sent a shaft of fear through his body. Fear he had to keep concealed from Olivia. She'd been so brave so far. He'd never loved her more. Once they got out of here he'd never let her go again.

"Post fourteen is down," he yelled. "We can't see thirteen." As he spoke he was calculating the time it would take to clear the tunnel. Unless Stavros had no one to help him. Then they'd never make it out in time.

"Are you alone?" Jack shouted. "Do you have the crew?"

The answer was unintelligible. It sounded like "See you soon," but that was probably just wishful thinking on Jack's part. Then there were no more words at all.

"He's a good man," Jack said. "No one better. He's seen it all. He knows what to do."

He couldn't see Olivia, but there was something about her silence that told him she was crying. He kept talking, trying to distract her from thinking the worst.

"Depending on the size of the pieces, they could have us out in an hour or two," he told her.

"This is the most dangerous phase, isn't it?" she said. He knew she was thinking of a dig on Cyprus they'd read about where a tunnel collapsed and the digger was buried alive. "Since the supports have failed, just the act of digging through the rubble could trigger an even bigger collapse."

"And the tomb gets the final revenge on the intruders. The curse of the mummy is just folklore, you know," he said.

"We don't know whose tomb this is."

"But I'm guessing you have an idea."

"Maybe. I just wish…"

"You'll have another chance at it. Once we get out of here and they redo the supports, the tomb will be there."

She didn't say anything until he got her talking about the discovery of King Tut's tomb in 1921, how it happened, what it meant and how the rumors of a curse circulated. She probably knew he was manipulating her, hoping to distract her so she'd forget she was trapped in a small space with time running out. Whether she knew it or not, she kept talking about it anyway. No wonder she'd gotten the Teacher of the Year Award.

"I don't see how they can call it a curse," she said, "when Carter lived until…"

Suddenly a dim light appeared at the top of the mound of rubble.

"Jack," Stavros called, his voice so loud it made them both jump. They watched a flashlight's beam poke through a face-size opening. "We have come."

Jack yanked Olivia to her feet. In the faint beam he saw her tear-streaked face, her dusty hair and he pulled her into his arms. "We made it," he said, hugging her to him.

She put her arms around him and buried her face in his shoulder. "I knew we would," she murmured, her voice trembling.

It took another half hour for the crew to clear and haul away enough rubble for the two of them to crawl through the opening to the main tunnel. When they came out, it was dark. No moon, no lights. No large crew. Only Stavros and the two other men he'd been able to rouse to come and help him.

Finally on solid ground, Olivia sucked in huge amounts of fresh air. Her legs were like rubber. Truthfully she thought they'd die in the tunnel. She just couldn't let Jack know how scared she was.

"I get worried about you, boss," Stavros told Jack, vigorously shaking his hand. "I tell my wife I have to come back. Make sure everything okay. Then I see blown breaker on generator and I don't find you anywhere. I think something wrong. Then start digging and get these guys to help me." He smiled broadly. "When I hear your voice I know you still alive."

Jack slapped Stavros on the back. "Good man," he said.

"Thank you," Olivia said in a small voice. She couldn't believe they were out. Safe. Alive. Thanks to this man who didn't have to come back to check on them. Who didn't get paid enough to save some crazy archaeologists.

That night she and Jack slept side by side in the tent. They didn't discuss it, he just dragged his sleeping bag to her tent and followed her inside. She was still shaking all over. She couldn't bear to be alone, couldn't stand to let him go, not for a minute. Before he fell asleep he threw one arm across her body, hugged her to him possessively and mumbled, "Don't forget about the honeymoon."

She lay there wondering if there really would be a honeymoon. Would he remember what he'd said in the tunnel? Would she? Or would cooler heads prevail? Tomorrow everything would be back to normal. Whatever that was.

When she woke up he was gone. His sleeping bag, too. What did that mean? She showered off all the residual dirt and went to breakfast. Every time Olivia tried to take a bite of her flaky cheese pie or bite into a ripe fig or sip the strong hot coffee at the breakfast table, someone asked her a question.

"How did you get down there?"

"Why were you down there at night?"

"What did you find?"

"Are you going back down?"

"Weren't you scared?"

She answered them all while keeping an eye out for Jack. Except for the question about what she'd found down there, she gave a purposefully vague answer. She wanted to check out that inscription before she told anyone. It was too important and too exciting a find to raise hopes before she was sure.

She hoped Jack hadn't gone back down in the tunnel. Even Jack wouldn't be so stupid. She finished breakfast and walked over to the excavation. There he was, shirtless in the early-morning sun, sweat glistening on his shoulders, his jeans hugging his hips, shovel in hand near the spot they'd come from last night. She felt breathless and dizzy just looking at him. Again the image of a classic Greek god statue came to mind. Only, Jack was real flesh and blood. Too real.

He waved cheerfully as if they were passing each other on a tree-lined California campus. As if they hadn't almost been buried alive only hours ago. He'd probably forgotten everything they'd said last night.

It was just as well. They'd both blurted things they wished they hadn't said. Things they didn't mean. They'd spoken as if it were their last chance. Their final words. Now that they were back on the surface, alive and well, their future was up for grabs again. Olivia felt exhausted just thinking about it.

In reality, nothing had changed. She was still worried about going back to real life at the end of the summer.

She still knew there was only one way to do it. Sell the house and get a divorce. Only one way to preserve her sanity, and that was to ignore Jack for now. Or rather to treat him like an ordinary colleague. Her going to Cal U was not going to happen any more than his returning to Santa Clarita.

She tried to get back to work sorting and cataloging broken pieces of glass and parts of ordinary clay amphorae, but her mind kept wandering. She kept taking deep breaths of air, fighting off waves of nausea, while she remembered the stale air in the tunnel and thought of what might have happened.

After lunch, as the sun hung high in the sky, and the temperature rose, the workmen took their siestas under the gnarled olive trees, while the staff huddled over their computers under the big tent. Jack found her leaning against a cedar tree on the cliff gazing out at the glassy sea shimmering in the sun.

"Let's go for a ride," he said, dangling a key in his fingers. When she looked puzzled, he said, "The boat. Robbins wants me to try it out. I can't do any work until they shovel out the tunnel and brace it up." He cocked his head and narrowed his gaze. "Come on, you look pale."

Nothing like someone telling you you look pale to make a person feel anemic. Jack, however, looked unbelievable gorgeous. His blue eyes were as bright and calm as the sea. He looked well rested, tanned and smiling. He'd fallen asleep immediately last night, while her mind wouldn't shut down and she kept playing over and over the near miss they'd had.

When she stared at him without moving, he put his hands on her shoulders and gazed into her eyes. "You're thinking about the tomb, aren't you? You know we can't go back down today or even tomorrow. So we're taking the afternoon off. I think we deserve it, don't you?"

She nodded. She couldn't think, couldn't even speak. She needed someone to make decisions for her. She needed Jack.

"You could use some sun," he said, gently tracing the outline of her cheek with his thumb. "And some fresh air. Go get your suit. Oh, you don't have one. Next time you're in town, be sure to get one. You'll need it for our long-lost honeymoon."

She didn't have the strength to argue with him. To tell him there wouldn't be any honeymoon. Today was different. He was right, they deserved a break. Besides, she wasn't much good at what she was supposed to be doing. Her mind kept wandering and she kept looking over her shoulder. She walked back to her tent and changed into shorts and a white camisole top.

Jack had started the motor by the time she walked out on the pier. He reached up to grab her hand to help her in the boat.

"Nice shirt," he said, raking his eyes over her breasts.

She felt her ultrasensitive nipples tighten under his intense blue gaze. The cami was suddenly too tight. Much tighter than the day she bought it in town. It must have shrunk.

She sat next to him on a leather seat behind the

wheel. The sun beat down on her bare shoulders. He turned a lever and the boat sped up. A fine spray of salt-water shot over the side onto her legs and she laughed. Maybe she was recovering after all.

Jack glanced at her and grinned. "No chance of getting seasick today," he said, surveying the area. "The sea's like glass and no sign of any weather."

It was true, the sea was smooth and the skies cloud-less. Still she felt a slight churning in the pit of her stomach. Nerves? Emotion? Or just her weak stomach?

"Where are we going?"

"There's an island over that way, called Kastemos. Stavros told me about it. I thought we'd check it out. Okay with you?"

She nodded. She didn't care where they went or what they did. Something had happened to her. Perhaps it was the brush with death last night or maybe it was the change in her relationship with Jack. No matter how often she told herself nothing had changed, it had.

"I'm in a different space today," she said. "I can't seem to think or concentrate. Maybe just a reaction to last night. What about you?"

"I feel great," he said, wrapping one arm around her shoulder. "You haven't changed your mind, have you?" He turned his head, cupped the back of her head with one hand and claimed her mouth with his. She blinked away the sudden tears that filled her eyes.

When she didn't speak, he said, "We're getting back together, remember?"

"Are you sure?" she asked.

"Of course I'm sure," he said. "I sent an e-mail this morning to my department."

Her stomach fluttered. "Already? You're really leaving?" Things were moving way too fast. She felt dizzy and disoriented.

"I'm coming back to live with you. We'll buy a new house. We'll make a new start."

Before Olivia could tell him things were moving too fast, they were rounding the island on their way to the tiny port city.

In a few minutes they'd docked at Kissani, and she breathed a sigh of relief to step on dry land. She'd never tell Jack, but she'd felt seasick even on that calm water. She was more sensitive than ever before, and she didn't want him teasing her about her weak stomach again.

Jack dug out his guide book, which suggested paying a visit to the local pottery school established for the preservation of the ancient traditional arts and located in the town square.

They walked hand in hand on a narrow road toward town. Olivia was dragging her feet. They'd only walked a quarter mile but she felt like she'd run a marathon. Was it her thoughts bearing down on her or was she just having a prolonged reaction to last night?

Jack was coming back. They were back together. Things were moving so fast she couldn't catch her breath. She knew one thing. Jack was decisive if nothing else. If he wanted something, he wouldn't hold back.

He'd sometimes teased her about "dithering." Which was what she called thinking things over. He made decisions quickly, and stood by them, right or wrong.

Inside the pottery school with its thick old walls, Jack asked what kind of pottery she preferred. She pointed to a blue and yellow vase that had the grace and beauty of the Gilded Age.

After he purchased the vase and some matching cups and saucers, and had them packed into a straw basket, they wandered to a monastery in a lovely seventeenth-century Venetian-style building. "You're still pale," Jack said with a worried frown. "Let's get something to eat."

They found a French bakery in a tiny lane behind the monastery with a grumpy baker behind the counter, who waved off their requests and insisted they order his famous fluffy quiche lorraine and have chocolate croissants hot from the oven with their coffee.

Jack watched with amused approval as Olivia dug into the warm quiche oozing with cheese and crumbled crisp bacon. "Didn't you have lunch?" he asked.

"That was hours ago and this is delicious. Are you going to finish yours?"

He slid his plate toward her. She polished off his quiche and then started on her croissant. "Thanks for bringing me here, Jack," she said, contentedly sipping her coffee. "It's just what I needed."

"Maybe we should rent a boat for our honeymoon, cruise the islands. Just the two of us. With stops at a bakery in every port of course."

"Sounds good, but…"

"You're not still worried about getting seasick, are you?"

"No, I'll be fine," she said with more confidence than she actually felt. "Or I'll get one of those patches for behind my ear."

She set her cup down. There were things to talk about. Decisions to be made other than where to take their honeymoon. "Does it seem a little strange to be talking about a honeymoon when yesterday we were through?" She propped her elbows on the small round table and leveled her gaze at him.

"Through?" He leaned forward and clasped her hands in his. "We were never through, Olivia. We were meant for each other and I knew we'd get back together again. Why do you think I got you to come on this trip? I never gave up. Did you?"

"Yes," she said. Now was the time to be honest with him. No more pretending she was fine when she wasn't. "You're amazing, you know. If you didn't have any hurdles in your way, you'd invent them. Because you're so darn good at overcoming them."

"You make everything worthwhile, Olivia. We're going to have a great life together. Even better than before. Better house, better honeymoon, better jobs. Because we almost lost it all, now we know what we want."

"Are you sure about that, Jack?"

"Of course I'm sure. I was an immature, selfish SOB when we met. You were right, I was thinking only of myself. Losing you shocked me into realizing what's important to me. It isn't a job and it isn't having kids. It's you. That's it."

Olivia bit her lower lip to keep it from trembling. Her eyes filled with happy tears. She felt a huge surge of relief. If Jack was sure, then she was sure. If he knew it would work, then it would. He kissed away her tears, and even the grumpy baker gave them a reluctant smile when they paid the bill and complimented him on his food.

They walked hand in hand along the sea wall as the sunset's rosy glow reflected off the water, passing a few tavernas, a few rooms to rent and finally reached a long stretch of rocks, pebbles and fine golden sand. Finally they reached the dock where their boat was tied up.

The sea was still glassy, but Olivia was sick again. So sick she threw up over the side of the boat.

"Maybe I shouldn't have had that second quiche," she said, weakly plunking herself down next to Jack again in the front of the boat.

"You'll feel better when we get back to Hermapolis," he said, smoothing her forehead.

But she didn't feel better. She felt worse. Just the smell of the fish soup simmering on the open fire for dinner, a soup she'd previously loved, made her run the other way. Instead of joining the group at dinner, she grabbed a bottle of mineral water, two aspirins for her headache, and dragged a canvas camp chair to the cliff above the beach. She wanted to be alone, but a few minutes later Marilyn joined her.

"You had a real scare last night," Marilyn said.

"You could say that," Olivia admitted.

"Well, 'all's well that ends well.'"

"Right. I hope they get that tunnel cleared soon. I want to go back down."

"Still think there's a tomb down there?" she asked.

"I hope so."

"Brave girl. We missed you at dinner," she said. "Jack says you're feeling a little woozy."

Olivia wished Jack hadn't said anything. "I had a late lunch. I'll eat an energy bar later."

Marilyn tilted her head and studied Olivia for a long moment in the waning twilight. "Maybe you're pregnant."

Olivia choked on a laugh. "I don't think so."

"Nausea, vomiting…"

"I was in a small boat this afternoon. I get seasick," she said tersely. If Marilyn only knew how ridiculous her suggestion was.

"When I was pregnant I was so sick…tired all the time, nausea, heartburn and sore, tender breasts. You name it, I had it. Makes you wonder why you ever do it again. But I did, four kids and…"

"Marilyn, stop. I'm not pregnant."

"Of course, it could be something else. Flu, Dengue fever or something worse."

"I'm fine. Really." Olivia stood. She had to get away from this well-meaning but meddling woman. But the world spun around and she quickly sat down again.

Marilyn stood there looking at her with an "I told you so" expression on her face.

CHAPTER TEN

THE NEXT day Olivia told Jack she had some errands to do in town.

"I'll come with you," Jack said. "I can't go back underground yet."

"I'm going shopping. You'd be bored."

He frowned and gave her a long look. She rubbed her palms together nervously. There was something wrong with her and he didn't know what it was. He'd spent last evening talking with Robbins around the campfire while Olivia retired early. When he got into his sleeping bag next to her in the tent last night, she pretended to be asleep, but she wasn't. It wasn't a good sign for someone who planned to spend the rest of his life with her.

He told himself to give her some space. That episode when the passageway collapsed had really affected her. He didn't blame her. They'd faced death down there. Being buried alive had been a distinct possibility, and they both knew it.

Olivia also had claustrophobia to overcome. And disappointment at not being able to get at the treasure that might be buried there. Then there was their future to think about. Exciting but problematic. At least for her. Not for him. He'd already decided to leave Cal.

There was no point insisting he go with her to town. When she made up her mind, she didn't back down. Instead he handed her the keys to the Jeep.

"You need anything?" she asked, obviously relieved he wasn't going with her.

"Just you. You're all I need." He cupped her chin in his palm and brushed her lips with his. Her lips were warm, too warm.

"Are you okay?"

"I'm fine," she said peevishly, avoiding his gaze. Then she quickly turned and went to get the Jeep. He stood there watching her drive away on the rutted dirt road until she disappeared and only a cloud of dust was left. He ran his hand through his hair. Later someone asked him a question about the length and direction of the excavation, but they might as well have been speaking Chinese.

When Olivia got back from town a few hours later, she left all her purchases in the back of the Jeep and hurried toward excavation site.

"Anyone seen Jack?" she asked.

No one knew where he was except for Elias, who was digging a hole in the ground with a pick. He pointed to the beach. From the top of the cliff she saw Jack sitting on the beach, arms locked around his knees and staring out to sea. She took a deep breath and scrambled down the path, small stones falling around her, skidding on the loose dirt under her feet.

When she reached the beach, Jack turned and smiled at her. A heartbreaking smile that made her ache inside.

He stood. "Did you get what you needed?"

She nodded. "Sit down, we have to talk."

He winced as if he expected a low blow. And she hadn't even told him what it was about.

"I hate it when you say that," he said.

They sat next to each other on the pebbly beach looking out at the azure sea and at small white boats bobbing in the distance. She sighed. Such a lovely, peaceful scene. It was too bad to inject a dissonant note. But it had to be done. She couldn't wait. Even though she'd been practicing all the way back in the Jeep, the words were now stuck in her throat and refused to come out.

"Maybe it's not so important, after all," he said after a few minutes had passed.

"Yes, it is, yes it is." The words poured out at last. "Jack, it's not going to work, you and I."

He scowled at her. "What do you mean?"

"It's been too long. Too much has happened. You have your life and I have mine."

"What you mean is you don't love me anymore," he said flatly. A muscle in his temple twitched.

"You could say that," she said carefully.

"I want to hear you say it," he said. "Otherwise I don't believe it."

"Love has nothing to do with it," she said. "We have to do what's right."

"What's right? I'll tell you what's right. That we get back together again. I thought we'd agreed."

"Maybe we did, but we were under a lot of stress. We thought we were going to die. We both said things we didn't mean. Now that we're alive, we can think more clearly."

"I *am* thinking clearly," he said, spitting the words out with his jaw clenched. "I never said anything I didn't mean."

She nodded. That was the problem. He'd said too much. He'd meant every word of it and he couldn't take it back, even if he wanted to and he didn't.

"Let's not make this any more difficult than it is," she said. "We've got a few more weeks left here. We've got a tomb to discover. We have other people around." She glanced up at the cliff. She wouldn't be surprised to see a group of their colleagues gathered up there, trying to hear what was going on, saying, "Are they or aren't they?" "Are they together or not?" But there was no one there.

"You want me to pretend everything's okay between us?" he demanded.

"Since no one knows where we stand it shouldn't be so hard. Just act the way you always have."

"I can't do that. I love you and I think you love me. I want you back. I'm prepared to do whatever it takes. Tell me what you want."

"I want you to forget what happened here. Forget we agreed to reconcile. It was a rash thing to do. We thought we were going to die. We said things we wish we hadn't.

Please, Jack." She swallowed hard. She would not cry in front of him. She couldn't let him know how she was being torn apart inside. She summoned every ounce of strength she had. She pressed her lips together and turned away from him. "This isn't easy for me."

"Isn't it? It looks like it is from here. It looks like something happened I don't know about. Why don't you tell me what it is? Then maybe I'll understand better. Until then why should I make it easy for you to say no? I thought we agreed we'd have no more secrets from each other. If we didn't agree, we should have."

She should have known he wouldn't go away without a fight. She had to make him understand. She had to, but she couldn't, not without telling him the truth. She knew him so well. She knew exactly what he'd do and what he'd say if she did.

The only way to cut this conversation short was to get up and go. That's what she did. She stood and brushed the sand off the back of her shorts before she climbed back up the steep path. She didn't look back, but she knew he was still sitting there, staring out to sea as the sun set and darkness fell over Hermapolis.

The good news was Jack avoided her just as she avoided him for the next two weeks. More good news was when she and the whole team got back down into the unblocked passageway and she deciphered the entire message on the stele.

In the year 293, month of Panemos, day 20, Alexander III, son of Apollonia and Arte erected this stile for the his mother Artemidoros.

She wanted to jump for joy, to shout and celebrate with Jack. Artemidoros was of royal birth, and her tomb would be filled with precious gems, coins and sculpture, as well as everyday items she would need in the next world. But Jack was somewhere else, at the other end of the tomb, carefully mapping the royal route.

When the burial chamber was finally opened a week later it was everything she expected and more. There were vases, statues and intricate jewelry. And that was just the beginning. Late that afternoon Dr. Robbins brought champagne to the site to celebrate. She looked around for Jack. At least he ought to be able to share this one moment with her, if nothing else.

Without him, the joy of a discovery of this magnitude fell a little flat. She knew he was mad at her, she knew she'd asked him to act as if nothing were wrong. She didn't mean he should treat her as though she had a communicable disease.

Inside the big tent, with shadows falling over the compound as the sun set over the sea, champagne was flowing. Congratulations rang out. From twenty feet away Olivia caught Jack's eye. He stared at her, hostility blazing in his eyes, and she finally looked away.

Jack refilled his champagne glass. He knew he ought to congratulate Olivia on her work deciphering the tombstone and finding so many relics, but he couldn't stand to get close to her and not demand to know what was wrong with her. It wouldn't do any good. She wouldn't tell him. She was just as stubborn as she'd ever been. He knew that shuttered look in her eyes, the way she stuck her chin out and bit her lip.

He realized finding this incredible tomb at last was a letdown, without being able to share it with her. That hurt. It hurt him to see her smiling and talking to the others, while he stood there forcing a smile and drinking too much champagne.

"What's wrong, Jack?" Marilyn said, holding a glass in one hand and her notebook in the other. "You look like you just lost your best friend. Or your wife. You two not getting along?"

"Not really," Jack said. Why pretend? The summer was almost over. Everyone was ecstatic over the results of the dig. Everyone but him. He couldn't put up a front any longer. Why should he?

"She feeling any better?"

"You'll have to ask her," he said gruffly.

"The first three months are the worst," Marilyn said. "I ought to know. Four in a row."

"What are you talking about?" he asked irritably, setting his glass on a nearby table.

"Your wife. She's pregnant, isn't she?"

"I don't think so."

"I could be wrong, but she's got all the symptoms. Nausea, vomiting, fatigue."

"She was seasick," Jack said.

"On dry land? Come on, Jack, sometimes the husband is the last to know."

Jack turned to look at Olivia again. She was wearing

a tight T-shirt with a college logo on it. Her breasts, small but perfect, now strained the fabric. His face reddened as a few pieces fell into place. He felt as if there were a fire in his chest. If he opened his mouth, flames might come out. He pinned Olivia with a sharp glance before she hastily turned away.

He told himself it couldn't be true. First, it would be a miracle. After five years of trying, she got pregnant after one night at the hotel? Impossible. Second, she would have told him. Third, third…

He stalked across the ground and roughly grabbed her arm. "We have to talk," he said.

"Not now," she said, a flicker of fear in her eyes.

"Now," he said.

He pulled her out from under the large tent. The air was warm, perfumed with the scent of harvested wheat from the outlying pastures. "In the Jeep."

He sensed her resistance. He could feel the tension in her body.

"What do you want to talk about?" she asked, dragging her feet as he pulled her along.

"You and me."

"There's nothing more to say." Her voice held a note of desperation.

"You sure about that?"

If she was pregnant and hadn't told him— No, that couldn't be. She wouldn't do that to him. Not after what they'd been through. The years of tests, the waiting, the disappointment. He opened the passenger door of the Jeep. With his hand on her elbow he boosted her into the seat and slammed the door shut. Then he rounded the front and got in.

Olivia laced her fingers together to keep her hands from shaking. Her mind was racing. She hadn't been physically close to Jack for weeks, and his presence set her nerves on end. The anger he felt for her was a palpable presence in the air. Of course he'd find out some day she'd gotten pregnant, but she hoped it would be months from now, when she was back at her school and he was at his.

"Do you have something to say to me?" he said.

He knew. He must know. But how could he, when she'd barely found out herself?

Afraid to test her voice, she shook her head.

"Are you pregnant?" he asked.

She tried to look away, but he framed her face with his hands and forced her to meet his gaze. She didn't answer for a long moment. She didn't need to.

"How could you not tell me?" he demanded, dropping his hands.

"I wanted to, but I couldn't. Knowing how you feel."

"You know how I feel? Then you know I'm mad as hell because my wife didn't tell me she was pregnant. That I had to hear it from someone else."

"Marilyn," she murmured.

"Yes, Marilyn. Tell me why. That's all I want to know. Why, Olivia, why?"

"Because you'd insist you really did want kids after all, when I know you've changed your mind."

"How could you possibly think I changed my mind?"

"You said kids would get in the way. You said you

didn't want to share me with anyone. You said it. Don't deny it."

"Wait, wait. I said those things because I thought we couldn't have them. I was making the best of the situation. Of course I want kids."

"I wish I could believe you, Jack, but I don't. What about when I asked you if you were sure you didn't want kids, and you said you'd never been surer. Were you lying then or now? Because you can't have it both ways."

"Then. I was lying then, okay? So shoot me. I'm guilty. At least I'm not guilty of hiding the most important thing that happened this summer, the most important thing in my life, from you. Did you think I wouldn't find out that you…that we…" He stopped midsentence, obviously too angry to say another word.

Yes, she knew he'd be mad; she didn't know how mad.

"And were you also lying when you said you didn't want to share me with anyone? Because if I'm correct, having babies means a whole lot of sharing."

"Whatever it means, we're doing it together. You, me and the baby. Our baby."

"I knew you'd say that. I knew you'd make the best of it, because that's what you do. But it's not good enough, Jack. You're faking it. I can tell. I can't live like that. You're going to stay at Cal and I'm going to stay at Santa Clarita with the baby. You said it yourself, a baby would just get in your way." With that she wrenched open the door, jumped out of the Jeep and stalked off across the field toward the happy celebration.

CHAPTER ELEVEN

THE DAY they left the island, the sky was cloudy, but it was smooth sailing on the ferry. Still, no one could forget their last disastrous trip at the beginning of the summer. Olivia stayed glued to the railing near the lifeboats, prepared to be sick or to board a lifeboat. But unprepared to argue with Jack again.

This time she wasn't surprised when he approached her. She wasn't pleased, either. She couldn't debate the issue with Jack anymore. He was just as sure they'd get back together, and she was just as sure they wouldn't. There was nothing more to say. A future without Jack loomed large in her darkest thoughts.

"About that honeymoon I promised you," he said.

"Don't worry, I won't hold you to it. It's not necessary."

"You mean because you're already pregnant?"

"No, because…it's just not."

"I always keep my promises. You know that. When we dock in Piraeus, a car and driver is taking us to Cape Sounio on the Apollo Coast."

"That's where the Temple of Poseidon is," she said

breathlessly. "I've always wanted to see it." What was wrong with her? She was planning to say no to whatever he proposed. She just didn't know it would be a trip to a fifth-century temple or that her resistance would melt as fast as an Italian gelato in the sunshine.

"I know that. We should be there by sunset, when the view is spectacular, framed by the white columns of the temple."

"Oh," was all she could say. It was better than no or yes. It bought some time while she thought things over. Though truthfully, she wasn't thinking straight. All she could do was feel. And her feelings were getting stronger by the minute. It must be her raging hormones. Or the sea air. Or Jack.

"We're staying on the beach at the Hotel Aegeon. In the lobby they've got amphorae crusted with barnacles and gemstones they found in the sea below the temple."

"Jack," she said breathlessly. "You've thought of everything." How could she say no to a man who'd thought of everything? She thought she could, but not when he looked like a Greek god himself, his hair windblown, his eyes so blue she couldn't tear her gaze from his.

"Except for your swimming suit. We'll have to stop and get you one."

"I, uh, I got one in town the other day."

"In case someone suggested a honeymoon on a beach somewhere?" he asked. "Mrs. Oakley, you amaze me. You're the one who thought of everything."

"You never know," she said with a little smile.

"Do you know now? Do you know I love you? That I'll never leave you again, not even for a day?"

"You'd better not," she said as the sun broke through the clouds. "If you do, I'm coming with you."

EPILOGUE

Two Years Later

SENSATIONAL SICILY!
ART AND ARCHITECTURE TOUR
JUNE 25—JULY 10
Tour leaders: Dr. Jack Oakley, Dr. Olivia Oakley
Santa Clarita University proudly presents a journey to the classical world of Sicily. As we circle this magical island, we will view the classical sites from the past while enjoying first-class accommodations and delicious Sicilian cuisine.

SO MANY lovers of ancient ruins signed up for Jack and Olivia's tour they had to start a wait list and turn some of them down.

"Do you think we should have mentioned the third member of our leadership team before we came?" Olivia asked Jack on the balcony of the Grand Hotel overlooking the water in the old city of Siracusa on the island of Sicily.

Jack glanced inside at his daughter asleep in the hotel crib and smiled. "Judging by her popularity with the tour group, we'd be even more overwhelmed with applications than we were."

"No one seems to object to her tagging along in your backpack or the stroller."

"Of course they don't object," he said, surprised she'd even suggest it. "I'd like to see them try."

Olivia grinned. Jack was the proudest, the most devoted father anyone had ever seen. If little Sarah wasn't around, he pulled out pictures of her. How could she have ever doubted he'd be this way?

"Not to mention the fact that she's cuter and smarter than any baby they've ever seen," he continued. "Did you notice how she focused on those frescoes on the cavern walls the other day? I could just tell what she was thinking. 'Were those painted before or after the Norman conquest?'"

Olivia laughed. "Jack, she's only one year old."

"She's already an adventurous traveler."

"And eater. She loves gelato and antipasti. Good thing, since we're going to be traveling every summer."

"It would be nice if she had a little brother or sister to share the fun with," Jack said, steering Olivia into the bedroom with his arm wrapped around her waist. "And even help us dig. You know parents get old, and they can be really boring."

"Speak for yourself. I thought you found me exciting."

"I do. I do. More every day." He closed the shutters to the balcony. "I adore you, Mrs. Oakley," he said, hooking the strap of her camisole with his thumb and brushing his lips against her smooth shoulder. "I can't believe you're still mine, all mine."

"Believe it, Mr. Oakley," she said with a smile brighter than the Sicilian sun outside. "For always and forever."

* * * * *

Turn the page for a sneak preview
of the first book in the new miniseries
DIAMONDS DOWN UNDER
from Silhouette Desire®,
VOWS & A VENGEFUL GROOM
by Bronwyn Jameson

Available January 2008
(SD #1843)

Silhouette Desire®
Always Powerful, Passionate and Provocative

Kimberley Blackstone didn't notice the waiting horde of media until it was too late. Flashbulbs exploded around her like a New Year's light show. She skidded to a halt, so abruptly her trailing suitcase all but overtook her.

This had to be a case of mistaken identity. Surely. Kimberley hadn't been on the paparazzi hit list for close to a decade, not since she'd estranged herself from her billionaire father and his headline-hungry diamond business.

But no, it was *her* name they called. *Her* face was the focus of a swarm of lenses that circled her like avid hornets. Her heart started to pound with fear-fueled adrenaline.

What did they want?

What was going on?

With a rising sense of bewilderment she scanned the crowd for a clue, and her gaze fastened on a tall, leonine figure forcing his way to the front. A tall, familiar figure.

Her head came up in stunned recognition, and their gazes collided across the sea of heads before the cameras erupted with another barrage of flashes, this time right in her exposed face.

Blinded by the flashbulbs—and by the shock of that momentary eye-meet—Kimberley didn't realize his intent until he'd forged his way to her side, possibly by the sheer strength of his personality. She felt his arm wrap around her shoulder, pulling her into the protective shelter of his body, allowing her no time to object. No chance to lift her hands to ward him off.

In the space of a hastily drawn breath, she found herself plastered knee-to-nose against six feet two inches of hard-bodied male.

Ric Perrini.

Her lover for ten torrid weeks, her husband for ten tumultuous days.

Her ex for ten tranquil years.

After all this time, he should not have felt so familiar but, oh dear, he did. She knew the scent of that body and its lean, muscular strength. She knew its heat and its slick power and every response it could draw from hers.

She also recognized the ease with which he'd taken control of the moment and the decisiveness of his deep voice when it rumbled close to her ear. "I have a car waiting outside. Is this your only luggage?"

Kimberley nodded. "I assume you will tell me," she said tightly, "what this welcome party is all about."

"Not while the welcome party is within earshot. No."

Barking a request for the cameramen to stand aside, Perrini took her hand and pulled her into step with his ground-eating stride. Kimberley let him, because he was right, damn his arrogant, Italian-suited hide. Despite the speed with which he whisked her across the airport terminal, she could almost feel the hot breath of the pursuing media on her back.

This was neither the time nor the place for explanations. Inside his car, however, she would get answers.

Now that the initial shock had been blown away— by the haste of their retreat, by the heat of her gathering indignation, by the rush of adrenaline fired by Perrini's presence and the looming verbal battle—her brain was starting to tick over. This had to be her father's doing. And if it was a Howard Blackstone publicity ploy, then it had to be about Blackstone Diamonds, the company that ruled his life.

The knowledge made her chest tighten with a familiar ache of disillusionment.

She'd known her father would be flying in from Sydney for today's opening of the newest in his chain of exclusive, high-end jewelry boutiques. The opulent shopfront sat adjacent to the rival business where Kimberley worked. No coincidence, she thought bitterly, just as it was no coincidence that Ric Perrini was here in Auckland ushering her to his car.

Perrini was Howard Blackstone's right-hand man, second in command at Blackstone Diamonds, a legacy of his short-lived marriage to the boss's daughter. No doubt her father had sent him to fetch her; the question was *why?*

* * * * *

Get swept away down under with the glitz and glamour of the Blackstone empire as Kimberley tries to determine the real reason behind her "reunion" with Ric....

Look for VOWS & A VENGEFUL GROOM
by Bronwyn Jameson,
in stores January 2008.

Silhouette®
Desire

When Kimberley Blackstone's father is presumed dead, Kimberley is required to take over the helm of Blackstone Diamonds. She has to work closely with her ex, Ric Perrini, to battle not only the press, but also the fierce attraction still sizzling between them. Does Ric feel the same...or is it the power her share of Blackstone Diamonds will provide him as he battles for boardroom supremacy.

Look for

VOWS & A VENGEFUL GROOM

by

BRONWYN JAMESON

Available January wherever you buy books

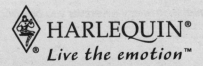

REQUEST YOUR FREE BOOKS!
2 FREE NOVELS PLUS 2
FREE GIFTS!

HARLEQUIN ROMANCE®

From the Heart, For the Heart

YES! Please send me 2 FREE Harlequin Romance® novels and my 2 FREE gifts. After receiving them, if I don't wish to receive any more books, I can return the shipping statement marked "cancel." If I don't cancel, I will receive 4 brand-new novels every month and be billed just $3.57 per book in the U.S., or $4.05 per book in Canada, plus 25¢ shipping and handling per book and applicable taxes, if any*. That's a savings of over 15% off the cover price! I understand that accepting the 2 free books and gifts places me under no obligation to buy anything. I can always return a shipment and cancel at any time. Even if I never buy another book from Harlequin, the two free books and gifts are mine to keep forever.

114 HDN EEV7   314 HDN EEWK

Name	(PLEASE PRINT)	
Address		Apt.
City	State/Prov.	Zip/Postal Code

Signature (if under 18, a parent or guardian must sign)

Mail to the **Harlequin Reader Service®:**
IN U.S.A.: P.O. Box 1867, Buffalo, NY 14240-1867
IN CANADA: P.O. Box 609, Fort Erie, Ontario L2A 5X3

Not valid to current Harlequin Romance subscribers.

Want to try two free books from another line?
Call 1-800-873-8635 or visit www.morefreebooks.com.

* Terms and prices subject to change without notice. NY residents add applicable sales tax. Canadian residents will be charged applicable provincial taxes and GST. This offer is limited to one order per household. All orders subject to approval. Credit or debit balances in a customer's account(s) may be offset by any other outstanding balance owed by or to the customer. Please allow 4 to 6 weeks for delivery.

Your Privacy: Harlequin is committed to protecting your privacy. Our Privacy Policy is available online at www.eHarlequin.com or upon request from the Reader Service. From time to time we make our lists of customers available to reputable firms who may have a product or service of interest to you. If you would prefer we not share your name and address, please check here. ☐

HR07

Inside ROMANCE

Stay up-to-date on all your romance reading news!

Inside Romance is a FREE quarterly newsletter highlighting our upcoming series releases and promotions.

Visit

www.eHarlequin.com/InsideRomance

to sign up to receive our complimentary newsletter today!